THE SHOWDOWN AT SAN BENITO

ROY CALVIN MOORE

Peak 1 Publishing, LLC

The Showdown at San Benito
by Roy Calvin Moore

For more information, address agent: JohnnyWelsh.com.

Published by
Peak 1 Publishing, LLC
P.O. Box 2046
Frisco, CO 80443

Book design by NZ Graphics

ISBN 978-0-9963078-7-1 (paperback)
ISBN 978-0-9963078-0-2 (hardcover)

Library of Congress Control Number: 2020900568

Printed in the United States of America

First Edition

This book is dedicated to the memory of
John Dawson Hamilton.

CHAPTER

I

Sergeant Major Stone spoke quietly to his commander: "Sir, General Lee is coming now." Colonel Welder quickly straightened his uniform and asked the sergeant to join him at the front of his tent to watch as the general passed.

John Welder was the youngest colonel in the Confederate Army. At seventeen, during his second year at The Virginia Military Institute (VMI), and shortly after the outbreak of war between the states, he left to join the Confederate Army. He had feared he would be too late, and the war would be over before he could see combat. All his classmates felt sure, too, that the war would not last more than a short time.

Son of a Virginia tobacco farmer, he had been raised in comfort but also with great discipline, with regular hours and schooling. Work on the estate was arduous, and his father had insisted he work beside the field hands as well as accompany him on trips to town.

One time he'd gone with him on a long trip to Washington, the nation's capital. Train travel was available, but his dad had insisted they travel by carriage. The Congress was in turmoil at that time, and there had been much talk of war. The Southern states were adamant, and there seemed to be no possibility of compromise.

When war did come, the elder Welder immediately joined the Confederate Army, taking more than twenty of his own men as well as half a dozen friends. He was given the rank of major in the Confederate States Army (CSA) cavalry and was killed in the first skirmish with Northern troops at Bull Run.

Young John, at VMI, had abandoned his studies and joined the CSA as a private in the cavalry. He was permitted to take his horse, Allheart, a magnificent six-year-old gelding. Thanks to his life on the farm, young John was an excellent horseman, had lived with firearms all his life, and was physically superb. Six feet, two inches tall, at seventeen he had not yet achieved his full height.

Determined to honor his father, John faced the enemy head on, leading his contemporaries in battle, oblivious to his own safety and fierce to the point of being foolhardy. Even though the young man had been in the thick of battle on several occasions, he had never suffered a wound. Each night he spent time praising God and giving thanks for his safety. Raised as a devout Catholic, John gave all credit for his safety to his creator.

A battlefield commission came after his second engagement at Ball's Bluff, Virginia, where he and his platoon captured thirty of the enemy. General P.G.T. Beauregard, the brigade commander, observed the young recruit in combat and ordered his immediate promotion to the rank of lieutenant. Rising quickly in rank due to his obvious leadership capability and his fearless conduct in combat, he was promoted to full colonel just three months before the end of the war.

Colonel Welder now stood as General Lee approached the camp. He could see the general mounted on the gray mare as usual, with a guidon riding to his right and half a horse length ahead and his adjutant and aide to his left. He had been waiting for Lee's return and knew that the war had probably been lost.

General Lee instructed his adjutant to assemble all officers, down to and including young lieutenant squad leaders. By the time the officers were assembled, it was almost dark. The general's remarks were brief, and the assembled officers were deathly quiet as he spoke. The war was ended, and there were no more battles to fight. He repeated the terms of surrender and instructed the officers to return to their units and brief their men. There would be a detachment of Union soldiers on the morrow to accept the surrender and offer parole to the men. After that ceremony, the men would be free to return to their homes.

It was dark by the time Colonel Welder returned to his tent. He finished the task of writing letters to the families of the men he had lost in battle. He had no way of knowing whether the letters would ever be delivered. The entire world seemed to be in chaos, and there was nowhere to go for answers.

He left his tent and walked the short distance to the hospital tent. Spending an hour among the wounded, he felt the suffering was almost more than he could bear. Doctors were working the best they could with no medicine or ether to ease the pain. Using strong enlisted men to hold down the wounded, they probed for lodged bullets, set broken bones, and removed limbs too badly damaged to save. With so many wounded, the doctors worked on those least damaged first; those not likely to survive were left for later. Several men lay on stretchers on the ground outside the hospital tent. John spoke to those who could hear him, holding a hand or giving comfort in any way he could.

Returning to the regimental headquarters tent, Colonel John Welder passed several campfires with men gathered around discussing their future. Sergeant Major Stone was talking to a group of enlisted men around a fire a few yards in front of the regimental tent. John joined them, and they all stood as he approached. "At ease, men. No longer any need for formalities. The war is over, and we are all on our own now. Make your way back to your homes and families. It's a sad time, and it's going to be rough going for a while. I'd suggest you travel in groups if you can. Three or four will be better than being alone."

For some of the young men, the thought of being all alone was worse than the fear of coming battle had been. All had been in more than one skirmish and most had survived large-scale engagements, but now there was fear of the unknown. The period of reconstruction could last for years. The unknown could last a lifetime. Most wanted only to return to family and friends, but some had no idea where to turn. Talk continued until near midnight before some started drifting off to try to get some sleep.

At three in the morning only Sergeant Major Stone remained to talk to the young colonel. Stone was slightly older than his colonel and had served loyally by his side for the past two years of the war. An outstanding noncommissioned officer, he had an unusual military bearing and a loyalty to his commander so fierce it verged on worship.

After some time, the two men spoke. "What do you plan now, Sergeant?" the colonel asked.

"I have nothing. I have no home and no place to go," Stone said. "I was a child in Atlanta and that city no longer exists. The home I grew up in is no longer there. All my family were killed, and I have no one other than this unit. I guess I'll go south away from these goddamn Yankees and try to find work as a lawman. I'm good with firearms and I fear no man. I'd make a good lawman. A sheriff or a sheriff's deputy."

"Yes," Welder said. "You have done a hell of a good job keeping our troops in line, and you could do the same for a town or a county. You'd make a good lawman. I have some land, but I haven't been home for two years, and I've heard from friends there's nothing on it. Everything has been destroyed or burned. It's south about a hundred miles, and I'm going there. I want to see for myself. Ride that far with me if you want."

"Thank you, sir. I'd be proud to ride with you and be of service any way I can. I don't see that I have any need to hurry, and two men together have a better chance than one man alone. You have a fine mount—my old horse ain't nothing like you ride, but she's a tough old Morgan and in good health. I've taken good care of her. I guess we have all we need with two horses, the guns, and enough hard tack to last a bit. I can be ready to ride as soon as we are dismissed. If you are ready, sir."

"Be proud to have you with me, Sergeant," Welder said. "You're a good man and I couldn't do better. I've done my duty the best I know how, and I don't know anything more I can do for the men. By the terms of surrender, as I understand them, I'm no longer in charge of the regiment anyhow. I'm a civilian and you are too. Don't bother with the 'sir,' and from now on I'm just John. You'll get used to it. We've got a lot to get used to in the next few weeks."

"Thank you, sir—uh, uh, John. And I guess I'm through with Sarge. From now on it's just Max; Max Stone. I sorta liked that Sergeant Major though."

The surrender was brief, and the defeated Confederate soldiers were permitted to keep one sidearm, one long gun, and a mount if they had one.

Chapter
II

The ride south was mostly through wasteland. Signs of the war were everywhere. Fortifications, abandoned trenches, breastworks of stone and logs, and, at times the stench of death, mostly from animals, since the bodies of fallen soldiers had already been buried in a marked-off area. There were few proper grave markers, mostly simple fieldstones and a few wooden crosses to signify the graves. Some names and occasionally a unit were carved in wood or scratched into a stone.

The Welder farm, Weldwood, was devastated. The mansion had been burned to the ground. Only slave stones used as the footing remained to mark its location. Outbuildings were gone without even a footing to mark where they had been. Trees had been cut to provide heat for men of both sides during the war. None of the great fruit trees remained—apple, pear, and nut trees were all gone.

There had obviously been a battle of some sort at the plantation because trenches and some log fortifications remained. The remnants of battle had been salvaged, and there was nothing of value left. Scavengers from the North were already in the village, seeking plunder of any kind.

John located a man seeking to buy land. Property of any sort was available for sale by impoverished locals unable to care for the land. Stripped of slaves to work the fields, there was no way to continue with the tobacco, corn, wheat, and truck crops of the past. The estate was listed in county records as four sections, almost three thousand acres.

It was almost a month before John was able to get a judge, appointed by the new governor, to certify John as the sole survivor and owner of the property. Surprisingly, the buyer offered more than John had expected to realize from the sale. Payment was entirely in gold coin because the federal dollar would not be well received in the South for some months, perhaps not for years. For the moment Confederate money was also still used for many transactions.

John knew that travel with that amount of gold was a risky venture and he discussed it with Max. "If word gets out that there is that amount of gold to be had, there will be blackguards eager to take it and willing to kill to get it. We'll both need eyes on the backs of our heads. I have no plans other than to go south and start a new life. Maybe on the Mississippi River. I always liked the water and a man could make a living working on the river. New Orleans might be good. We can get on the river at St. Louis and take our time. See how we like it. Try Natchez and New Orleans. I know Natchez was just about destroyed, so there may be some good opportunities there. Main thing is, we need to act fast. Decide what we want to do and do it before someone else."

Max nodded in agreement. "I think the two of us can handle any scum that thinks they are big enough to take anything from us," he says. "I'm pretty handy with a six gun or with a long rifle and meaner than a snake in a knife fight. I'd feel good riding with you."

With no more agreement than that, the two prepared for the long trip. Provisions were hard to come by; food was a problem and what was available was of poor quality. Ammunition, however, was plentiful. Signs of past battles were frequent and more common than land unscathed from the recent war. Scavenged from these battle-fields, there were cartridges by the case and many guns gleaned from the fallen soldiers.

The local people they encountered were shy and reluctant to have anything to do with strangers moving through. Many of the surviving solders of the Confederate Army were desperate men and out of necessity were willing to rob or steal to survive. John learned quickly to speak from a distance, introduce himself, and explain his intentions.

Almost all that he approached clutched a weapon of some sort; a flintlock long gun was most common, but there were also more recent models of rifled long guns and shotguns. Even if they had no gun, the residents would clutch a long knife upon the approach of a stranger. "Hello, friend," was usually John's first greeting as he approached a local resident. Stopping twenty paces or more and showing both empty hands, he and Max could see the stranger relax a bit.

Explaining their mission, John would say, "We're Confederates, friend. Headed south as far as we can go. We're short of necessaries and would be pleased to pay for anything you can spare, and we can pay in gold. Flour, salt, salt pork, dried beef or goat. Anything we can carry, we'd be interested."

Some would ask them to just move on. "Nothing here for you, stranger. I got less than enough to feed my own." Other times the home-owner was friendly. After some conversation, they would ask the travelers to get down and sit a spell, offering water and occasionally something to eat. Boiled corn ground up and simmered for an hour or more over a fire was the most common offering.

As summer progressed and they moved farther south, the land became more normal, with stretches where no signs of the war could be seen. Gardens were growing, and there were occasional undamaged houses and outbuildings. The men rode for an hour or two between resting the horses, and they stopped from time to time for a half day or more when finding good grass for the horses to enjoy. Seldom finding shelter, they usually camped by any water source they happened upon.

In early August, they came across the Natchez Trace west of Nashville, Tennessee, far east of their intended route. Not interested in any particular destination, they were not concerned but decided to follow the trail because it was well traveled. Many Confederate soldiers moved down the trail, seemingly of the same mind: Just go south as far as possible to get as far from the Yankees as possible.

John had heard of the fierce siege and battle at Vicksburg, Mississippi, so they left the trace at Jackson and traveled west. "We'll see what opportunities there are in Vicksburg," he said. "It's been destroyed, but it will come back. Perfect spot on the river so there has to be a town there."

The weather was great, and there were already signs of recovery as they arrived in Vicksburg. A garrison of Union soldiers was stationed in the town, and John was careful to avoid contact. They were seldom friendly and openly displayed their control over the citizens.

Death, literally and figuratively, still hung over the town. Livestock killed during the last battle had not finished the process of decomposition and filled the air with the horrible odor of death. Even some human remains, not properly buried, had been dug up by scavenging varmints desperate for anything to eat.

The atmosphere was so depressing John chose to move on, farther south. Finding an old barge set to haul coal to New Orleans, the two arranged passage with the understanding they would sleep with their mounts on deck and share food with the three-man crew. The space ahead of the open cargo hole was limited, making it necessary to tether the horses for the three-day journey to New Orleans, the owner making it clear he had no plans to make any stops before arriving.

CHAPTER
III

First item on the agenda when the barge docked on the east bank of the river south of town was finding a bathhouse to rid themselves of the grime of three days on the barge and a clean stable for the horses. Riding up the river, the two came to a livery with reasonable rates for stabling the horses and feed. As a bonus, there was a hotel of sorts just a short walk away. The owner offered hot baths and sleeping rooms plus boardinghouse meals for those able to pay.

The owner was a one-armed man, who they learned was a captain in the CSA who had lost his arm early in the war and had returned to his home in New Orleans. He and his young wife had acquired the hotel during the heat of the siege of New Orleans—when property values were at an all-time low. They had survived the siege without damage and were forced to serve the enemy for the duration.

After his wife left the room, the owner informed the men that ladies of the were night available for a dollar charge if they took one of the ladies to their room. The dollar would be split evenly between the hotel keeper and the lady in question. The men declined, being more interested in a hot bath than in female companionship.

The hotel was comfortable, and the food was better than any they had enjoyed in months. The next two weeks, the men talked to as many local people as would spend time with them, learning what was needed. Shipping seemed to be most in demand. There was more cargo coming from the North down the Mississippi than ocean shipping could handle.

Neither man was enthusiastic about becoming seamen, but the city was wide open for opportunities in saloons, prostitution, and gambling. John had a talent for cards: for playing the odds in any poker game as well as being able to discern telltale signs in opposing players. He was almost always able to tell when a player was bluffing and won many a hand by calling a bluff when he held a good hand.

Over the two weeks he had won more than two-thousand dollars when, unexpectedly, a professional gambler accused him of cheating. The man felt sure John was able to read the cards and must have known what was in his hand. The gambler pushed back from the table and stood, pulling aside his coattail to reveal a holstered revolver. "You're cheatin', mister. Keep your hands on the table and stand up. 'Fore I search you—one of you men count the cards and stack them by suits."

John remained seated and could see Max sitting quietly at the bar. Max moved slowly as he lifted his own pistol from its holster. It aroused no attention as everyone in the room watched the men at the table. "Unless you got cards up your sleeve, there better be fifty-two cards on the table and none missing," the gambler said.

John countered, "I got no cards on me, and I called because I don't think you got a winning hand." John spoke with both hands palms down on the table, his cards pushed toward the center of the table. "You find any marks on any of them cards, I ain't seen it. I got no shiner and ain't nobody working the table with me," he said. "You touch that hog leg, you'll be dead before it clears leather. I got no reason to kill you. It's the man behind you with his pistol in his hand that will do the killin.'"

The room was silent and all in the room, other than the gambler, turned to look at Max, who was still sitting quietly, gun in hand. The gambler did not turn but blanched noticeably. "So, you got someone reading my cards for you?" he asked.

"You know damn well you ain't never flashed a card since you sat down. You're a better gambler than that," John said. He eased his chair back from the table. Moving slowly, he put more weight on his hands and rose to stand facing the gambler. "Max," he said, "you can put yours away. I'll take care of this man myself if he has any more questions."

The gambler was relieved because in his mind he was sure there was a gun pointed at the back of his head. By then, a player had separated the deck into four rows, stacked so all cards were in order and visible. No cards were missing. The man counting the cards spoke: "I think you made a mistake, mister. Ain't no cards missing from this deck, and I can't find a mark on any of them. Mr. Welder here ain't no professional, but he damn sure is one of the best card sharps I've seen play the game. He beat you fair and square so you better pick up your money and leave while you can still walk."

Still angry but unable to see how John had cheated, the gambler lowered his gun hand and raked the little money he had left from the table into his other hand. "I ain't done with you, mister. I think you cheated but I don't know how. You best get out of these parts 'cause I'll be lookin' for you." He turned and left the saloon.

A man got up from a table and joined him as he walked out. Max heard the older man speak quietly as they walked past. "Go back and get six men. Tell them to be here by noon tomorrow," the man whispered. Max followed to the swinging saloon doors and watched as the two men walked down the muddy street. Sure they had actually left and were not lying in wait, he returned to talk to John.

"I don't like it, John," he said. "We'd be sitting ducks with men waiting to ambush us. I ain't one to run from a fight, but this ain't no fair fight. With a long gun, they could pop us from anywhere before we ever saw them."

John didn't count the money he picked up from the table, and the four remaining men stayed seated, ready to continue the poker game. "Thank you, gentlemen," he said. "Sorry about the interruption. I think he was just a sore loser and a bad card player."

As they returned to the hotel, John made plans to leave New Orleans. "I ain't seen nothing here that looks all that promising," he said. "Texas is new and wide open. I'd like to look it over and see what it has to offer."

CHAPTER
IV

The cattle boat from New Orleans was not clean, but most of the manure from the last load of cattle out of Texas had been removed and cargo was stacked to the capacity of the barge. The horses were tethered on deck, provided with hay and given a couple of pounds of grain the first afternoon and late morning on the second day.

The duo had acquired an additional animal—a sturdy mare mule, four years of age and sound as hickory. The mule was used as a beast of burden, relieving their mounts, which had become over-loaded with their personal possessions.

The port of Indianola was in sight by midafter-noon, but it was nearing dark before the barge was tied to the wharf along with a number of other vessels, mostly barges but also a couple of small sailing craft.

Both men were tired because there had been very little comfort and little sleep during the night. Neither man was accustomed to the rough ride and constant wallow of the barge as they made their way to Texas. What sleep that did come was troubled by thoughts of all that could happen to the barge in the open water of the Gulf of Mexico. Time was money to the captain and his course had been a straight line, which was riskier than following the shoreline, although it took several hours less time to make the trip.

John and Max were not the only passengers. Twenty or so men and two women were also aboard, as were their belongings and half a dozen horses. Most were poorly dressed and clearly looking for new homes in the new state of Texas. Most talked of the stories they had heard of the land available for pennies an acre and even free land in places to attract settlers where labor was in short supply.

John studied the settlers as they moved their meager belongings off the cattle barge onto the dock. All those people moving in, eager to start new lives in a new land. There must be opportunities here that none had even dreamed of. *Where does my destiny lie? John pondered. Commerce? Bringing in goods from the North where manufacturing was centered? Could I use this mass of humanity in some way? Cheap labor by those unable to fend for themselves in a hard land? What service would be in great demand? Transportation? Retail trade? Land acquisition? Banking? So many opportunities but what direction to take?*

Unlike most, John had arrived with a substantial amount of capital to invest. Max was eager to move inland. He had not enjoyed the trip by water from New Orleans, and the stench of the cattle barge seemed soaked into his bones. He wanted most of all to get a hot bath and wash the smell from his clothes. He thought, *I'll even wash down the horses.*

The horses fidgeted nervously on the dock when first led ashore, unaccustomed to the firm deck after the days on the unsteady boat. Maud, the mule, was calm and clearly happy to be on solid footing once again. She stood quietly as the men watched those going ashore.

Almost immediately following the departure of the last passenger, the dock workers started assembling the chutes to direct the livestock from the holding yard onto the barge. Provisions for the crew were easily loaded, and within two hours of docking the barge was cast free to return to New Orleans.

Two hundred animals, in panic and fear, kept up constant bellowing, rearing and butting in a vain attempt to survive. With a reasonable crossing, the barge would arrive with a hundred and ninety or more living animals. A rough crossing and the captain could lose as many as fifty. In a short distance the pens would become so slick with manure and urine that cattle could not maintain their footing; they'd fall and be trampled by those still standing.

The crew, accustomed to the suffering of their cargo, were unaffected and hardly noticed the downed animals or their plight. John had read of a method to manufacture ice and wondered whether it would be possible to slaughter the animals, pack them in ice, and ship them to markets back East with little or no loss.

The two men found room for the night in the home of a local businessman with a large clapboard house. They had met simply by asking directions to a hostelry where they could also have the horses cared for. Mr. Bronson was a large man of more than ample girth, well dressed and quite friendly to the newcomers.

"You men don't look like the usual settlers comin' through Indianola," he said when approached. "I have some contacts hereabouts and could likely give you directions to find whatever it is you are looking for.

"Come over to my place on Lavaca Street. The two-story white house. I got a stable and men to care for your horses. An extra room where you'd be welcome to spend the night. Happy to have visitors able to speak English."

They visited briefly and John accepted the invitation. "Thanks, Mr. Bronson. We appreciate it, we are getting as far as we can from the Yankees."

"Confederate soldiers?" Bronson asked.

"Yes," John answered. "Both of us went through the whole thing. Max has a couple of scars to prove he was a hero, but I got off scot-free."

They had a pleasant evening, and Mr. Bronson was a treasure trove of information. He knew where the best land was and what was most needed in this new land. He said, "We need men willing to work and not looking for a handout. Men interested in building a country and using this great state to build and prosper."

Time passed quickly, and before anyone realized it, it was after midnight. The men shook hands all around and took their leave. The beds were excellent, with actual featherbed mattresses. John and Max were more exhausted than either had realized. They slept soundly, but Max was up early to watch the sun rise slowly over the water from an excellent vantage point out the upstairs window of their room.

"What a beautiful morning," he said to the sleeping John Welder, not wanting his friend to miss the sight of the rising sun. After a good breakfast prepared by Mr. Bronson's housekeeper, the pair accepted his offer to spend a few days with him as they searched for other accommodations and decided whether to stay in Indianola or move inland.

John liked the bustle of the small port city and all the activity going on. Every day a hundred or more travelers moved through, looking for a new life in the new land of Texas. John watched with interest the movement of cattle through the port. There were large stockyards where ranchers brought their cattle to market. There was a large surplus and the barges were loaded to capacity as fast as the cowboys could move the herds. Most were small independent operators with barges capable of hauling a hundred or more cattle.

Some were quite large and capable of hauling as many as five hundred at a time.

With such a high volume of livestock going through the port, John felt sure he could make a fortune if he could find a way to get into the business of moving the cattle to market. He was impressed by the huge losses suffered due to animals lost in transit. As much as twenty percent of the cattle brought to the port failed to arrive safely at markets in the East.

"Max, there's a man down in San Antonio who is making ice with a machine. A Mr. Daniel Holden. I'm going down to talk to him and check it out. There may be a better way to ship this beef to market."

The men traveled together on horseback to San Antonio and spent some time with the gentleman who was starting his ice plant. The process was only in the development stage, so much of the equipment in use was of his own design and manufactured locally. Nonetheless, the plant was producing ice in uniform fifty-pound blocks and was capable of producing more than a hundred of the blocks each day, which was enough ice to cool a small barge filled with beef long enough for travel to New Orleans. John was excited by the prospect of starting a new industry, shipping frozen fresh beef to market.

CHAPTER
V

The men returned to Indianola and set to work. To accomplish their goal of shipping a barge a day full of frozen beef, it would require more of an investment than their cash on hand and finding financial backing was a problem. Mr. Bronson was well known and successful in his own right. He introduced John to the local banker who in turn introduced him to the banker in Victoria, about forty miles inland.

Between the two banks they were able to agree on an arrangement that would provide a line of credit for the construction and operation of a combination slaughterhouse-ice plant that could fulfill contracts with prospective shippers. John was able to retain full ownership with liens on all the property and any cattle, equipment, and supplies as well as an obligation to supervise the entire operation. Should the operation fail, John would lose everything he owned. On the flip side, should he succeed, he would be one of the wealthiest men in Texas.

With the proceeds from the sale of Weldwood, that would not be an insignificant amount invested. Cheap labor was plentiful, and construction of the ice plant proceeded quickly. With the help of Mr. Holden, the equipment for ice making was brought in and set up. By early in the spring of 1866, the plant was producing ice. For the amount of ice John wanted, it was necessary to produce ice twenty-four hours a day, seven days a week. With production up to eight tons of ice a day, it was time to test his plan to ship refrigerated beef.

Leasing a barge from an independent operator, John had the barge cleaned and added bins for the mixture of ice and beef carcasses. The bins were twelve feet by twelve, and ten feet deep. Thirty bins in all with each bin holding more than two tons of beef sides as well as a layer of beef parts as the top layer; hearts, tongues, brains, liver and testicles. The workers loading the bins stopped at dockside to weigh the beef while the scale keeper listed the quantity and beef parts. In the town of Port Lavaca, a sawmill processed timber from

East Texas which came by barge from the forests above Galveston Island. John contracted with the mill to deliver all their sawdust to the port at Indianola, where he built a warehouse for the purpose of storing large amounts.

The beef was packed with a layer of sawdust on the bottom, ice next, and then a layer of beef sides. The beef was placed so there was little space between sides. Another layer of ice came next, then more beef until the bin had room for a final layer of ice; all was covered by a foot of sawdust before the two barn-door-size lids were closed.

The first shipment received an excellent report with no spoilage and the beef tasting the same as freshly killed. Soon the new "cold beef" was in demand, with meat-packers bidding up the price to unheard-of levels. Beef that cost just over six cents a pound to process and ship was bringing over thirty cents a pound at dockside in New Orleans.

Because of the demand, they determined the best way to market the beef was by auction at dockside. Each buyer bid on a full bin—three-and-a-half to five tons of beef. The buyers wanted to buy the beef off the barge in a package they could move more easily, rather than unpacking the bins at dockside. Crates would have to be the solution in order to transfer the meat from the barge to wagons. John found the change to crates was expensive but well worth the trouble.

The beef was of such quality the word quickly spread, and buyers from farther north came to New Orleans to bid for the beef. There seemed to be a never-ending demand and John struggled to increase production, working the slaughterhouse in two shifts to run continuously. He would not have any but a minimum crew in the ice plant work on Sundays.

The operation of the slaughterhouse and icehouse was running smoothly. Max was a good supervisor and the lady in the office did an outstanding job of documenting every facet of the business: payroll, billing, collections, scheduling, filing, etc. Every scrap of information was carefully cataloged and filed. There was little for John to do other than sign payroll checks and make various other payments to suppliers and shippers.

One cattle buyer, Mr. William Tipton, was a man born to ranching who knew cattle better than anyone in Texas. Well-paid and honest, he worked well with the ranchers from Corpus Christi to Houston. They appreciated his knowledge and respected his honesty in offering the best price in the market for prime cattle. He could spot sickness in the herd at a glance and frequently warned growers of a problem they would not have suspected.

CHAPTER
VI

Residue from the slaughterhouse was loaded on a barge to be dumped far offshore, but the local cotton farmers felt the offal would make good fertilizer for their crops. They would send open wagons to the plant and load the offal to haul as far as ten miles to spread on fields. The demand became so great that after a time there was no need to dump the residue offshore. It was easy to tell from a distance when a farmer had just spread the offal due to the swarm of birds feeding on the smelly mess.

Land in Texas was selling at unusually low prices, and John felt it was time he invested some of his accumulated cash on hand. Rather than pay the loans from his creditors, he began to invest the extra money in land before the supply dwindled and prices went up. There was the risk that much of the best land would be taken unless he moved quickly.

Leaving Max in charge, he headed by horseback for Victoria, traveling at a leisurely pace and looking over the land as he traveled. There were few settlers on the Texas plains between Indianola and Victoria. Any house he came upon, he would stop, ostensibly to rest his horse but in fact to visit with the homeowner and learn as much as possible about land for sale in the area.

It was during this trip that John happened on the home of a widow with significant land holdings her husband had acquired before his death—seven sections of rangeland some ten miles east of Victoria. The land was just about the only asset. The small two-room house was little more than a shack with chickens in the yard and an outhouse out back.

Mrs. Beck was friendly and offered the traveler cold tea. She also invited him to have dinner with her and her daughter. Charlene was seventeen and a lovely blond-haired girl. She was rather shy and added little to the conversation.

They had a late dinner of pinto beans and cornbread. There was an ample supply of milk and butter, as Mrs. Beck kept a milk cow that she milked twice each day. The widow was willing to discuss the sale of her land holdings but had little knowledge of land values including hers.

"Look it over and tell me what you think I should sell for," she said. "Spend the night, and tomorrow Charlene will show you the place. She's lived here all her life and knows every hill, gully, cactus and what few livestock we have. There are rattlesnakes, too, so be careful. Some javelinas, but they are more scared of you than you are of them. Had some Injun trouble when we came here but haven't seen an Injun in five years or more."

John spent the night, sleeping in the front room on a quilt spread on the floor, his own saddle roll as a pillow. The widow was up before sunup and had milked the cow before John awoke. The sound of the skillet on the old woodstove roused him from sleep, and he went outside to relieve himself and wash his face at the yard pump.

When he returned, Charlene was sitting at the dining table as her mother served breakfast of white gravy, biscuits, eggs, and grits. Charlene said, as she ate, "Mom says you want to look over the farm? I'll ride with you and show you what we got. There's probably a thousand acres or more, so it will take most of the day."

Charlene, even though she knew what land was on the ranch, had little concept of how much land there actually was. It was just where she grew up, where she had lived all her life, so she knew where the boundaries were from childhood. There could have been no better guide.

She dressed in men's slacks and a shirt for the ride and wore a floppy Stetson hat with her hair up beneath the hat. By the time the sun was full up, they rode out with a picnic lunch in saddlebags on the girl's horse. John had tied his bedroll behind his saddle and had full saddlebags below. His long gun was resting in a saddle scabbard under his right leg, within easy reach should he need the gun on short notice.

The house was near the north side of the ranch; they rode south for a mile or more before turning west, riding for a while down the western boundary of the property. Near noon, judging by the sun, they turned east toward a small valley that Charlene knew.

In a short time, they rode down a steep hillside to a freshwater creek flowing northeast toward the Guadalupe River, coming to a large bluff to the south with a small waterfall carving a pool below it. They dismounted and Charlene spread a sheet for their picnic as John relieved the horses of their saddles, leaving them where they could reach the water and graze the green grass alongside the flowing water.

He joined Charlene and they enjoyed small talk as they ate. She told him about life growing up in the barren Texas plains. The death of her father when she was only twelve. The struggle to run the ranch with her mother and trouble constantly with drifting cowboys looking for stray cows or plunder of any kind. Some asked for work but most only asked for a bite to eat to sustain them on their travels.

Even when she was twelve, the cowboys would eye Charlene (as well as her mother) with obvious lust in their eyes and double entendres in their conversation to make it clear that they would enjoy the attention and affection of either of the ladies, mother or daughter.

Mrs. Beck always carried a revolver in a gun belt, and none of the cowboys or drifters had become overly bold in their attempts to gain sexual favors. At seventeen, Charlene had never known the pleasures of love with a man, yet she was not immune to the feelings aroused by the sight of a handsome cowboy.

After lunch, John lay back on the sheet and rested his head, face covered by his hat as protection from the sun. The morning in the saddle had taken a toll, and he quickly drifted off in sleep. After twenty minutes or so, he was awakened by the sound of splashing water. Charlene was in the clear pool enjoying the feel of the cool water on her body as she bathed. "Come on in," she said, as she raised from the water enough to expose her young breasts to John.

"God! Lady!" John exclaimed. "You got no clothes on."

"Don't matter," she replied. "Ain't nobody within five miles, and it's just the two of us. I won't look if you come in."

John could not refuse. He was still young and healthy with all the passions of a normal man. He simply had denied himself these past years as he concentrated on rebuilding his fortunes. Checking the horses to be sure they would not wander off, he quickly stripped and joined the girl in the tepid water.

It was like entering a tub for a nice bath, and the water was remarkably clear. Under the cliff was a small overhang with exposed ground above water level. After some playful splashing and each attempting to dunk the other, the girl swam the short distance to the ledge below the cliff. She climbed out of the water and stretched out on the smooth ledge.

John joined her, sitting beside her and marveling at the perfect body before him. He placed a hand on her side and knelt to kiss her. She did not resist, pursing her lips to receive his kiss and hooking her arm around his neck. The kiss lingered and her passion rose to a dangerous level as John encircled her young body and pulled her to him.

Suddenly, she broke free and scrambled into the water. Laughing as she swam, she moved quickly to the far side of the pool and climbed from the water. John followed, diving rather than splashing into the water, and swam swiftly in an attempt to catch Charlene before she reached the edge of the pool. Too fast for him, she leapt from the water and ran toward the horses.

Halfway to where the horses were tethered, she tripped on a tree limb in the grass and fell. John reached her before she could recover from the fall and dropped down beside her. As she sat up, he embraced her young body in his arms and brought her face to his, kissing her with all the passion stored in all his life in search of this moment. She yielded and offered herself to him.

"Please, be careful," she whispered. "I've never been with a man before."

John would not, could not, admit that it was his first experience with a woman as well. That was not expected, and had he said so, she would not have believed him. The first experience was more than either had dreamed it could be, and their passion knew no bounds. They were like animals in the wild with their frantic mating.

Passion spent, they both lay back in the soft grass to rest. After some time, Charlene spoke: "Mama told me that it would hurt when I did that the first time. Wow! It didn't hurt a bit. It didn't do nothing but feel good. More than good! It was like dying and going to heaven. I couldn't even think, it was so good. Thank you, John Welder. I don't even feel like the same girl now. I just want to run and fly and shout to the world how good I feel."

John watched with a satisfied look on his face as the girl jumped to her feet, racing to where the horses were tethered. Grabbing the reins of her horse, she leapt to his bare back like a young Indian buck mounting a war horse. Digging in her heels, she slapped the horse's neck with the reins and sped off across the plain. John mounted his horse in the same manner and raced after her. Both young people, totally nude, rode bareback, racing across the valley floor.

CHAPTER VII

L eft in charge of the icehouse and packing house in Indianola, Max had an easy time of managing the business with the help of their very competent secretary. Mrs. Barnes was also the office manager, with three additional staff to manage the growing business. What a change in such a short time. Busy days had more obstacles than either man had expected and frantic days when things failed to go smoothly.

Pressing on and ramrodding through every obstacle, they had built a good business and were now processing between two hundred fifty and three hundred cattle a day, sending a barge six days a week to markets in the East. Some went to New Orleans and north as far as Illinois up the great Mississippi River. Others went around the tip of Florida and up the East Coast to markets from Jacksonville to as far north as New York. Soon they would be going farther, to Boston and even to Maine.

And then, a catastrophe—one of the large freezer compressors seized. It would take weeks to replace the compressor, and the maintenance supervisor said there was no possibility of repairing the damaged compressor. They were not out of business, as there were still four working compressor units, but their capacity to ship would be reduced by close to a third.

To ship with less than a full load of ice was to court disaster. They could easily lose a complete load of beef should the barge run short of ice. The price of the new compressor, nearly seven thousand dollars, was more than Max was willing to commit to on his own.

John must be consulted. "I'm going to tell John," he told the secretary. "I don't want to commit to that much without his knowing. I'll be back by tomorrow night. Just keep things going until I get back."

Knowing approximately where John had headed in his search for rangeland, Max packed provisions in saddlebags and was on the trail to

Victoria within an hour. Within two hours, he had learned John was talking with the widow Beck and located her place.

As he approached the house, the widow was working in her garden. Always leery of anyone traveling through, she raised up, checked the location of the long gun at the edge of the garden, and walked toward it. Stopping some distance from the garden, Max introduced himself: "Howdy, ma'am. I'm Max Stone, and I ride with John Welder. There's been some trouble and I need to talk to him."

"Get down and have a drink of water, Mr. Stone," she replied. "Looks as if your horse could use a little rest as well. Take him there to the stock tank and sit a spell."

She picked up the long gun and followed him to the stock tank, taking the handle of the water pump and pumping fresh water. "Wait a bit and it will be cooler."

Max helped himself to the long-handled dipper hanging on a post near the well and caught a cup of water. It was cool and refreshing, and he had another before stopping. "Yes, Welder's here," she said. "He's interested in buying me out. I sent my daughter to show him what land I got. They'll be back by sunset, so you may as well sit and relax."

"Nothing I'd like better, ma'am," Max said, "but I really need to see John and get back to the plant before dark if I can. If you'd just point me in the right direction, I can track them pretty well."

"They headed south along the west side of the ranch. There's a nice watering hole seven miles south on Coleto Creek that Charlene knows about, and I think they would stop there for a while to rest the horses and have something to eat. I'd guess you could probably catch up to them there if you hurry."

Max thanked the widow and mounted for the ride. The horse moved at a slow trot, and as he approached the creek, Max guided the horse to the high ground overlooking the valley. If they were in the valley, he would be able to see them for two miles or more from that vantage point.

Some upheaval in ancient times must have created that cliff. Rising some two hundred feet above the valley below, it was a sheer drop to the bottom of the cliff. Max dismounted as he approached the cliff edge and looked out over the valley. It was a clear East Texas day and he could see forever.

There were cattle far downstream from the cliff but no riders or horses. Ironically, the couple he was looking for was below him at the base of the cliff. He located them, and he started to hail John but stopped short. The two were in the clear water, playing like children.

He watched for a moment, went to his horse for a brass telescope he had taken from a fallen Yankee during a battle, and came back to take a better look at the pair. It was only then that he realized they were both naked. *Damn! I better not bother them now or John will kill me*, Max thought. *I'll wait until they get out and get dressed and then ride down.*

He sat back, rested his head on a large rock, and waited. At times he could hear the laughter of the two as they played and an occasional squeal from the girl. The next time he looked through the telescope, the two were in the grass near the horses. Max witnessed the coupling of the young lovers and caught his breath upon seeing the young girl in all her glory. *MY GOD!* he thought. *What a beautiful creature!*

Becoming aroused himself, he turned away, ashamed of himself for witnessing such an intimate event between his friend and the girl. The next time he looked, the two were riding downstream away from him, and for an instant he thought he should ride to catch them.

Looking once more through the spyglass, he saw they were both riding bareback, still totally naked. They would be back for clothes and saddles in time. Max relaxed once more and waited.

After no more than ten minutes, they returned, riding side by side now, laughing and teasing each other as they rode. John dismounted, dressed quickly, and saddled the horses, prepared to continue the tour of the ranch.

Only then did Max mount his horse and make his way to the valley floor. John and Charlene were a mile or more east before he overtook them. Calling John's name as soon as he was within hailing range, he finally caught up with them. Max made no mention of the activity he had observed from his place high on the cliff.

"John, we've had a breakdown at the ice plant," Max said. "Glad I caught up with you so quick. It's going to cost more to fix than I felt like spending without talking to you about it."

Without dismounting, the two discussed the breakdown of the compressor and the options. They could get a compressor from New Orleans in a week, or it would take three weeks or more to get one from Atlanta. Downtime at the plant would more than outweigh the added cost, so John told Max to go ahead and telegraph the dealer in New Orleans to ship the compressor.

Rather than return to the ranch house with John and Charlene, Max turned his horse toward Indianola. It was late by the time John and the girl arrived at her home. Her mother wasn't there so must have gone to Victoria. "I'll start supper if you want to rest a while. It's been a long day," Charlene said. "Turn the horses loose and sit a spell."

By the time her mother returned, Charlene had the meal almost ready, so the timing was good. "I had a good day, but all that time in the surrey gave me a sore behind," Mrs. Beck said.

They made small talk while eating, and as Charlene cleared the table, Mrs. Beck went to a cabinet and returned with a bottle of brandy. "I've saved this for a special occasion, Mr. Welder," she said as she sat the bottle on the table. "I've spent the day thinking of your offer and pretty well made up my mind to sell you the place if we can come to terms. I'll make you an offer and you see what you think of it.

"I'll speak plain because I don't want any misunderstanding. I've had a hard life here and I'm getting past my prime. I need a rest and I'm tired of going to bed dead tired every night. The ranch ain't worth much 'cause it ain't been kept up like it aught."

She poured a couple of fingers of brandy into two drinking glasses as she talked. Taking a sip from her glass, she continued: "I'll sell you the ranch for less than what it would bring on the market but with some stipulations. I've lived here most of my life and this is home to me. I don't want to leave home and try to find someplace else at my age, and Charlene ain't never had no other home in her life."

By now Charlene had finished with the dishes and joined them at the table. "You ain't so much interested in a home as you are in the land, so this is what I have in mind. You leave me to live out my days in this house with a little patch of land to keep some chickens, pigs, a milk cow—and some room for my garden. And you can do what you like with the rest of it. I'll not be a bother and not try to tell you what you can do with the rest of the place.

"Other than what livestock I have here at the house, you can have the cattle you find on the place. I'd guess there are twenty head or more. Hardly worth your trouble to round them up."

Pausing to study his face, Mrs. Beck looked John in the eye. "Now for the last," she said. "My daughter is full grown now. The cowboys driftin' through here ain't nothing to dream of for a son-in-law."

She watched his face closely as she made the proposition: "You are a man of substance, educated and with more spunk than ten of them worthless cowboys been after my daughter. So, as part of the deal, you take Charlene to be your wife and I'll sell you the place with the requirements I've told you. You can have it for five thousand dollars."

John was stunned and it showed on his face. There was silence around the table as both John and Charlene tried to absorb what Mrs. Beck had suggested. The thought passed through his head: *God has found a way to save me from my sinful ways. This is His way of making it right, what we did today.*

He was at a loss for words as he tried to gather his thoughts. That was not at all what he had expected as part of the deal. The thought of becoming a married man had not even crossed his mind before today. He could only stammer and stutter for a moment.

"Uh, uh, um. I'm flattered you would think I was a good enough man for your daughter. I don't hardly know what to say. Gosh! I'd have to ask her. Umm, uh, wow! Charlene, what do you think about what your mom just said?"

The girl was blushing fiercely. She could not look at either of them. She hid her face in her hands and sat silent, thinking. After what seemed to all to be a long time, she spoke: "Are you askin' me to marry you, Mr. Welder? You don't need to marry me to buy my mom's land. That don't have to be part of the bargain."

Mrs. Beck started to speak, but before she could, John responded: "I would be proud if you would agree to be my bride. I've not seen a woman like you since before the war. I'll admit I have been too busy to think about getting married or being a family man, but I sure could never do better with what little I've got to offer. If you'll say you'll marry me, we'll seal the deal here and now. There's nothing I'd like more than to marry you. I sure enough need a woman in my life. Will you marry me?"

Charlene studied his face. *Was he sincere or was he feeling guilty about what they had done just six hours earlier down by the waterfall? Was he asking her just to be able to buy the ranch? How could he come to love her knowing she had just proved she was a loose woman?* Her mind was in a whirl and the thoughts got all jumbled up together.

"If that's what you want, Mr. Welder, I'd be happy to call myself Mrs. Welder. Yes! Yes! I'll marry you if you'll have me."

Mrs. Beck watched her daughter intently. She had raised the girl and knew her as well as anyone can ever know another person. Something was amiss. *Just the excitement of the moment? The suddenness of it all? A whole new world for the girl?*

Her response and the look she gave her mother were not what Mrs. Beck had expected. But then she didn't really know when she had made the proposition what either of them would think or how either would respond. She knew Charlene would do anything she was told to do, but Mr. Welder had no obligation to take the girl.

It was the girl she cared for, far more than any attachment to the land. She had recognized for the past three years the passion in the girl and knew full well that she could not protect her forever from the men she came in contact with on the infrequent trips to Victoria or from the drifters passing through.

"That's it then, Mr. Welder. If you'll shake hands on it, we have a bargain. I ain't in no rush and we can do the deal legal anytime you like. I been banking at the bank in Victoria since we come here, so they can do all we need to do to make it legal. They even have my papers there."

The two shook hands and the girl got up to hug her mother. That was the first time in months she had actually hugged her mother. Then she went to John. "I'll make you a good wife, Mr. Welder. I promise. I'll be a better wife than you ever dreamed of." She only held his hands. No hugs or kisses, but she looked deeply into his eyes.

"Starting now," John said, "there will be no more 'Mr. Welder' when you speak to me. From this moment on, it will be 'John.' It's OK if you say 'Mr. Welder' when you're talking to others about me, but when we are talking, it's just 'John.'"

Once more John spent the night on a quilt in the front room of the house, but he was not really able to sleep. He was sorely tempted to steal into the girl's bed after Mrs. Beck was sleeping soundly but dared not. *God is watching and knows what is on your mind*, he thought to himself. After a long prayer to thank God for his good fortune and beg forgiveness for that moment of weakness by the pool, he tried to sleep.

Sleep would not come, and he was up before the sunrise over the Gulf of Mexico. Mrs. Beck had not slept well either and was in the kitchen starting a fire in the woodstove by the time he had gone outside to relieve himself. Coffee was boiling in the pot when he returned. He sipped coffee as his soon-to-be mother-in-law made breakfast.

He had almost finished eating when Charlene came from her room, looking disheveled and sleepy-eyed. She had not slept well either and was still in her nightgown. She passed through the kitchen without a word, walking out the back door to the outhouse some fifty yards from the back porch. Before returning to the house, she pumped water at the well, washed her face, and smoothed her hair the best she could.

Without further ado, the deal was done. The three left early for Victoria and went first to the bank to start the necessary papers to transfer the title to the land. Leaving the banker, Bud Galloway, to do the paperwork, they went to City Hall across the street for the license to marry.

A trip to the old Catholic Church at the south edge of town followed, and the kindly old priest invited them into the rectory. A young Mexican nun offered them refreshments and then left them to talk to the priest. After a lecture, which seemed overly long to John, concerning the sanctity of marriage and his expectation that they would become regular members of the congregation, the priest performed the marriage ceremony.

With all the activity, they had not taken time for dinner and all were ready for a good meal. The priest gave them directions to a café on River Street that served both Mexican and Anglo food. The wedding dinner was brief because the hour was late.

By the time they were finished, it was after sundown and the return to the ranch was completed well after dark. All were exhausted after the long day. With the formality of the wedding ceremony deeming it proper, John joined Charlene in her bed as they settled down for the night. Mrs. Beck smiled as she listened to the activity in her daughter's room. Content with the events of the day and with a feeling of relief at the selling of the land, she slept deeply.

There was much to do, and John left the next morning to return to the ice plant. He explained to Max what had transpired, and they made preparations to turn the operations over to a plant manager. They found a capable man who had been a loyal and productive employee from the time of construction of the plant to accept the position.

John would need Max at the ranch to supervise the construction of a home, quarters for ranch hands, and handling pens for the livestock, plus start the operation of a working ranch. Both would return to the ice plant from time to time to check the operation and solve problems that were inevitable. John had larger plans and needed contacts at the state capital. He would be able to take the train now from Victoria but planned to take his horse along in the cattle car.

CHAPTER
VIII

M r. Galloway at the bank was happy to write a letter of introduction for John. That document opened many doors in the capital, and John was accepted easily into the company of both politicians and businessmen. John rented a room in the home of the widow of H.H. Telfner, and due to its easy access to the capital, he maintained the residence even when not in town. Mrs. Telfner was pleased with the arrangement, too, since little was required in the way of cleaning and upkeep.

John became well known around Austin in a short time and was frequently invited to dine with those in positions of power in the state. Not infrequently he was introduced to visitors from the nation's capital on government business involving federal programs in Texas.

Arriving back at his apartment on a Friday afternoon, John was introduced to Mr. Joseph Telfner, brother-in-law to the widow Telfner. Joseph and his brother, H.H., had traveled together from Italy as young men. Young, ambitious, and well-educated, they were the very men that Texas needed to grow and prosper. H.H. became a prosperous lawyer with offices in both Austin and San Antonio. Joseph used the abundant cheap labor to build things—buildings, bridges, roads. Difficult projects were his forte, and he had done well, adding to the considerable fortune he had brought with him from the old country.

As a pastime, H.H. had enjoyed gambling with others in the Austin area and occasionally in San Antonio when he had business in his offices there. Three capable lawyers conducted business in San Antonio, and H.H. had both a partner and two associates in the office in Austin.

During a game in a guest room at the Capitol Hotel, which stood across the street from the state capitol, H.H. was shot and killed by a disgruntled loser. The game had been seven-card stud and H.H. had a jack and two eights showing. The other man had two nines showing and two nines in the hole.

Betting was heavy. On the last card H.H. drew the fourth jack, and the two nines showing bet ten thousand dollars. Realizing he could beat any possible hand his opponent might have, H.H. called the bet and raised the man ten thousand. Now there was more than thirty-five thousand dollars in the pot.

Feeling confident that H.H. held a full house, which his four nines would beat, the man—although he had no more cash on hand and could not easily cover any marker—offered to bet his land holdings, valued at five thousand dollars. The land, eight sections north of Fort Worth, was easily worth more than five thousand and H.H. called the bet.

Upon revealing three jacks in the hole, the man, in frustration and despair, drew his pistol and shot H.H. in the chest. "He's a cheatin' goddamn card sharp!" the man exclaimed. "I saw a jack fold in that hand," indicating the hand to his left. "We ain't playin' with a deck with five goddamn jacks." The three remaining players, having already pushed back from the table in a scramble to avoid the shooting, were silent.

The man reached and turned over the folded hand to his left. There was no jack in the hand. Confused, he shook his head and nervously looked around the room. "Maybe it was that hand?" he said and turned the second hand to his left that had folded. No jack. Now, totally frustrated and confused, he quickly turned over the hand to his right, frantically searching for a fifth jack that did not exist. In desperation, he turned over the remaining card in the deck with the same results.

It was a clean deck of cards, and he had killed an innocent man, H.H. Telfner, winner of the pot, which contained nearly fifty thousand dollars and the marker for title to eight sections of land.

Thus, the widow Telfner was not left destitute. Renting rooms in her home was simply a way to enjoy the company of others. Her brother-in-law was in town working with friends in the capital to permit his company rights to land for a railroad between Houston and Brownsville. This was an ambitious undertaking that would rely on the Land Grant Act of 1864 to finance its construction. The state would guarantee sixteen sections of land, more than eleven thousand acres, for each mile of rail constructed and approved by state inspectors. It would be the largest single land grant since the huge grants by the government of Spain in the 1700s.

This was the kind of project John was interested in. He got along well with Joseph, and Joseph was pleased with the enthusiasm John displayed. There was room for another in his company. "We need men of vision," Joseph said. "Men willing to take risks, but more important, men able to make things happen. You've done well with the cold beef and shipping. I have heard only good things from those I know in Victoria and Port Lavaca. We need capital. Keep in mind that you could lose everything if you invest in this and it all falls apart. Natural disasters, war, who knows what the future could bring?"

John knew that this single undertaking could be the fulfillment of all his dreams or it could be his downfall. Recalling his despair at the surrender of General Lee, John knew well the feeling of loss. To join this undertaking, he would have to invest every cent of his small stake left from the sale of Weldwood—plus what he could put his hands on. He decided to divest his holdings in the Indianola company completely, borrow to the maximum against the ranch, and bet it all on this venture.

John stayed with Charlene at his mother-in-law's during the time he spent at the ranch, but more and more of his time was taken up with political affairs in Austin and some trips to San

Antonio. Work was not completed on the house on the ranch, although it was progressing swiftly under Max's guidance and Charlene's insistence that her child should be born in "his" home.

Finally, after months of well executed labor, the house was inhabitable, and John and Charlene were able to move in, even though workmen were still constantly traipsing in and out. Charlene was immediately comfortable in the new surroundings and was there for more than a week before she felt the first indication of the pending birth. John sent a rider to Victoria to bring Doc Mills. During that era, a birth at home was common and normally attended by a midwife.

This being Charlene's first child, John insisted there be a doctor present, and Doc Mills was the most respected doctor in that part of Texas. Accustomed to house calls, he did not protest when the rider informed him that Mr. Welder had requested his presence for the birth. In the early hours of the morning, he delivered a perfect baby boy. The housekeeper, a middle-age widow of Spanish descent, assisted the doctor.

Charlene insisted the child be named the same as his father. John was happy to accept the honor. He suggested the middle name be Max to honor his good friend and partner. Further, he insisted that he never be called Junior, only by his given name of John. In practice he was frequently referred to as Little John until well into his teen years.

Following the birth, John asked all to join him in the great-room, where he offered thanks to God for the safe delivery and birth of a beautiful son to bear his name. By the time it was necessary for John to return to Austin, the child was sleeping through the night and Charlene had returned to her regular routine, supervising details of the home construction and overseeing the house-keeper, Mrs. Esteban. Though her given name was Maria, it was never used around the home. It was always Mrs. Esteban.

John was satisfied with the progress at the ranch and with Max, who was doing an outstanding job of managing the thirty to forty cowhands, wranglers, and cooks. The number changed almost daily, with a cowboy deciding to move on or a cowboy wandering by looking for work. Most were turned away when obviously in poor health or after some conversation demonstrated they were incapable of performing the necessary work.

A lucky find was a middle-aged Mexican man who wanted work as a cook. John let him demonstrate his culinary talent, and the man served a dinner for the household: John, Charlene, Max, Mrs. Esteban, and the new girl Charlene had hired to assist Mrs. Esteban. The meal had a strong Mexican influence and was quite spicy with a liberal amount of peppers, hot sauces, and garlic. It was the best meal John had enjoyed since leaving the plantation to enter the Virginia Military Institute. There were no complaints around the table and the man was hired.

Though his job was to cook for the workers on the ranch, he could be called in to cook for the family should an event require a special meal. Mrs. Esteban, who did the normal cooking for the family, was happy with the arrangement since she dreaded cooking for company, not knowing their particular preferences in food.

John was now spending more time in Austin than at the ranch. Max had comfortable quarters in the building built to house the ranch hands, which was only a short distance from the Welder home. Charlene frequently called on him to help with any problems that arose and came to depend on his advice and help more than her husband's. Even when John was at home, it was not uncommon for her to summon Max to care for some problem around the house or grounds.

John had not yet returned to the marriage bed following the birth of his son. In his prayers at bedtime, he asked the Lord to let him return to relations with his lovely wife. Knowing that his purpose was to produce another child, he was eager, but given no sign from God, he held off. Even the obvious and frequently embarrassing displays of affection from Charlene failed to over-rule his strong religious conviction that intimate relations were only for the purpose of procreation. For now, he was content to spoil the boy child and hold him at every opportunity. The frequent smiles from the child were a delight to John, and he spent as much time with the boy as business would allow.

CHAPTER
IX

In the fall following the birth of his son, John was in Austin working with several contacts in government whose goodwill he needed to pass legislation favorable to the rail industry. This was the growing and indispensable transportation system vital to the growth and prosperity of the state. He made the decision to stay through the winter months since there would be a plethora of social events at which there would be the opportunity to influence those in the legislature.

It was during that period that a hurricane moved ominously up the Texas coast from the Gulf of Mexico. The storm clouds thickened all afternoon, and by evening the wind was blowing in gusts up to nearly fifty miles an hour. Thunder became almost continuous and lightning strikes came closer and closer. By dark the winds were fearful with almost continual thunder and lightning strikes.

On the ranch, the curtains were pulled and the house made ready for the coming storm. Charlene was concerned for the safety of her young son and checked his room every few minutes. The small room was joined to the master bedroom through a large pocket door, a door with two parts that slid into the wall on either side of the opening. With the parts open, it was simply an arched opening.

By late evening Charlene was shaking with fear. She rang for Mrs. Esteban. "Go get Max. Tell him I need him NOW! I fear this house will not stand. Hurry!" Mrs. Esteban wrapped herself in her pullover raincoat, a heavy canvas cover with slits for her arms and a drawstring around her throat. She had difficulty fighting the fierce winds as she made her way across the open area.

Max was in his room, and she pounded on the door to make herself heard above the almost constant thunder. Max had been lying in bed waiting for the storm to pass. All that could be done to protect the livestock and buildings had been done.

"Come quickly, Señor Max," she said as soon as Max opened the door. "Mrs. Welder needs you.

She is afraid the house will go. She sent me for you. Please come quickly!"

Max quickly dressed and pulled on his boots. "Wait," he said. "I'll go back with you. You will be safer holding onto me." He closed the door behind him, took her hand in his, and started across the area between the two houses.

The danger now was being hit by blowing objects and debris. All manner of things were in the air, with boards and trash large enough to be deadly projectiles. They moved as quickly as possible to the main house through the kitchen door, which was nearest to the ranch hand house.

Without hesitation, Max ran up the stairs to the master bedroom. Charlene was waiting at her door. As he entered, before he was able to speak, she threw her arms around him. "Thank God!" she exclaimed. "I was so scared. Why does John have to be gone at a time like this?"

She was shivering in his arms, and Max held her close to comfort her. "Now, now," he spoke as he cradled her in his arms. "We'll be alright. It's just a little hurricane, and John couldn't know it was going to hit us here."

She calmed and embraced the comfort of his strong arms. "Thank God, you're here," she said.

"I didn't know what to do. Hold me. Hold me tight." It was a clumsy moment for Max. He had given her a hug in the past on special occasions, but hugs like a brother gives a sister.

Her face nestled in his neck, she hugged him as tightly as she could. This was more than a sisterly hug. "You feel so good," she whispered. "You are so strong, Max. I could always count on you. You're like the big brother I never had."

Neither knew how long they embraced like that, just inside her bedroom door, before she was calm enough to relax. "Come, sit with me," she said as she took his hand and led him into the room. There were chairs, but they were on either side of the bed, and she wanted him close for comfort. Leading him to the bed, she sat and pulled him down beside her. "Stay with me, please. Stay with me until it stops."

Again, Max was uncomfortable but could not deny her, so he sat on the bed beside her. Again, she wrapped her arms around him and nestled under his arm. "I feel so much safer with you here. I just knew I was going to die. I was so scared!"

Max had never experienced such closeness with her before, and he could not ignore the warmth of her body. It could have been a combination of the fury of the storm and the closeness of her body, but whatever possessed him, he was starting to become aroused. Charlene was now beside him, clinging.

He had seen her once in all her glory and knew well what a beautiful creature she was. Without warning, she roused, pulled his face toward her own, and kissed him. As one, they fell back on the bed as they continued their embrace.

It was not something Max wanted. He had never permitted himself to even think of such a thing, but here with this beautiful creature in his arms, in her bed, with the storm raging outside, he had no control. She made no move to discourage him and helped as he removed her gown.

All was lost. Max quickly removed his own clothes as she made room in the bed beside her. Their lovemaking was as fierce as the storm that raged outside. It was the first time since the birth of her son, four months before, that she had felt the caress of a man.

After the act, they were both exhausted and lay in a lover's embrace, face to face, and fell into a deep sleep. It was almost daybreak before Max stirred, confused for a moment by the woman beside him. Then he recalled what had transpired. "Oh, Jesus," he breathed. "What have I done?"

Being as careful as he could, he pulled his arm from beneath the sleeping woman and got out of bed as quietly as possible. Gathering his clothes, he moved barefooted to the door, left the room, and dressed in the hallway to the stairs. Carrying his boots in his hand, he crept down the stairs and toward the kitchen door to the outside.

He failed to notice that Mrs. Esteban was in the child's bedroom, tending to him in his crib. The door to the landing was slightly ajar. Mrs. Esteban could see Max getting dressed, picking up his boots, and moving toward the stairs.

It was clear that Max had spent the night in the great house. She accepted that he had spent the night with her mistress. Why else carry his boots to more quietly leave the house? Only a guilty person would find that necessary, she concluded. She spoke to no one regarding the observation and treated it as a loyal employee should, putting it out of her mind.

CHAPTER
X

Negotiating with the lawmakers in Austin, John felt it imperative that he stay in town until the details were worked out regarding legislation favorable to the railroads. Between John and Joseph, they were able to convince enough lawmakers to pass the bill. The state of Texas would grant sixteen sections of land to the company for every mile of rail built and approved by state inspectors.

Looking to the future, Joseph contributed generously to the campaign fund for Edmund Davis, who was running to fill the office of governor. Mr. Davis was promised that the company would employ a substantial number of black men during construction and later as workers for the railroad. This indeed proved to be a good investment in the future, since Mr. Davis followed Governor Pease in the office.

Now came the time for heavy investment in construction equipment and land surveying. And hiring lawyers working with the courts to enforce the "right of eminent domain" granted by the state, when necessary, to seize railroad right-of-way along the proposed route. At times, owners would be reluctant to comply with court orders and required the presence of the local sheriff to enforce the orders.

It would be over a year before anything other than a short spur was built. That spur, little more than three miles of track, was used for training construction workers and assembling railroad equipment.

John's work with the legislators, representatives from steel companies, and manufacturers of all manner of rail-related equipment had consumed him completely. He was surprised to realize he had not been back to the Welder ranch for more than six months.

Even though a social life was necessary to maintain good relationships, it was the least favorite of all his activities. Despite this, John planned a gala event at the ranch to celebrate the progress made on the new venture, and plans were finally set for the last week of January.

The minutiae of building the company and starting actual construction had kept John busy during all his waking hours. He was sorely grieved about missing the holiday season at home with his wife and child, but the business had to come first, and the holiday season offered too many opportunities to cement business contacts with the hierarchy in Austin.

Charlene was clearly pregnant and had no idea how she would be able to convince John that he was the father of her child. She considered an abortion but that was an extremely difficult thing to do without seriously endangering her health. No doctor to her knowledge would perform the necessary procedure to terminate the pregnancy. There were Mexican midwives who would perform the abortion, but her fears dissuaded her from seeking them out.

She had not revealed her condition to John and had no idea how she could face him when he returned home in January. Her thoughts raced. I should have gone to Austin immediately following the stormy night with Max to spend time with John and expose myself to him in the marriage bed. Should have. Could have. Didn't. Why? Too late now.

Her mind was constantly in turmoil as to how she could possibly face John. Max was just as distraught but could not comfort her. They could run away he told her. They could just run away and change their names. They could be Mr. and Mrs. Smith in the Oklahoma Territory.

At a total loss as the day of the gala—and his boss's return—neared, Max finally rode to the shack at the cow camp on the southern end of the ranch. There was a rudimentary bunkhouse there where the cowboys slept and ate. Little more than a shelter from the weather, it did have rough bunkbeds and bare mattresses. Max figured he'd hide out there until he saw how the situation played out.

At the ranch, it was as Charlene expected. John was aghast. His face was ashen when he witnessed her condition. "How long has it been? How many months along are you?" he demanded.

She could not look at him and covered her face with her hands. "John, dear John! I am so ashamed," she sobbed. "I missed you so! I needed you so much!" She collapsed on the couch in the great-room, consumed by grief and embarrassment.

"Tell me," John demanded. "Who's the son of a bitch that did this to you? I'll kill him. I'll hang him at sunrise tomorrow. He'll have all night to know he'll hang at daylight."

"Please, NO!" she cried. "It was my fault. It was me. Please don't blame him. I was the guilty one." She knew it was futile to withhold his name. John would know whether she told him or not.

There was no way she could keep this terrible secret. "It was Max." It was scarcely a whisper. "It was Max, but it was not his fault. I enticed him. I almost forced him. I was so scared in the storm, and I needed someone so." She was finally able to confess all, and it seemed to take a terrible load off her mind. "You are always gone! You spend all your time in Austin."

She turned suddenly on the offensive, forcing him to share in the blame. "You think it is easy? Stuck here on the ranch with no one to love me? No one to hold me? I'm not a nun! I'm a woman! DAMN YOU! I'm a woman!"

John stormed out, walked the short distance to the bunkhouse, and roused the first cowboy he saw. "Get mounted. Go find Max Stone. Bring him here. Tonight! I want him in my office in the big house tonight!"

There was no need for the cowboy to ask why. The ranch hands had been talking for some time about the condition of the mistress and the prolonged absence of her husband. No one knew for certain, but their guess was good. Max was the number one suspect.

The cowboy quickly pulled on his boots, grabbed a slicker, and headed for the corral containing the remuda. Within minutes, he was mounted on a gelding and riding south. The most likely place to find Max was obviously the range shack on Coleto Creek. He let the mount pick its own way through the cactus and mesquite but spurred it on with frequent slaps of the quirt in his right hand. He covered the distance in less than an hour.

Max was not surprised. He knew that John would be home, and he now was prepared to face him. He saddled his own horse, leaving his gun belt in the bunkhouse along with the rifle from the saddle scabbard. He would face John and take whatever it was he had in store for him.

It was near midnight by the time they reached the ranch house. Max dropped the reins to his horse and spoke to the cowboy. "Leave the horse saddled. I don't know how long I'll be."

With that, he entered the house through the front door and went directly to John's office. The door was closed, but he could see there was a light on. He knocked lightly on the door, hesitated, and then tried the door. As the door opened slightly, John spoke. "Come in, Max." He sat behind his large desk, and that made it immediately obvious to Max this was not to be a friendly chat but strictly business.

"Good to see you, John," Max said as he walked across the office to face him. He stood, soldier like, before the desk waiting for John to speak.

"Max, it's good that you were not here when I arrived. My first thought, when seeing what has happened in my absence, was to kill," John said. "But I've had a couple of hours now to settle my thoughts. I've always thought of you more as a brother than a partner or friend. You have been more than a friend since we served together in the war. I've never doubted you for a minute … until today. Now you've let me down."

John paused, studying Max for an expression. There was no change as Max stood at attention, except he looked John straight in the eye rather than straight ahead as a soldier would. He sensed that John had not finished what he had to say, so he made no effort to respond, waiting to hear what his punishment was to be.

"I knew from the day I met Charlene that she was possessed by the devil, yet I have prayed for her day after day in hope that her behavior would change. I'll admit, I found her appearance lovely. I even thought of having another child with her. But I now see that she is an evil woman, consumed by lust she can't control. I know first-hand the evil that consumes her, so I believe without asking and without you telling me that she used you. I know without you telling me that you are not responsible for what happened. I don't think there's a man alive who could resist."

Max took a deep breath. His shoulders drooped slightly, so he was not standing as stiffly as he had been, but he still stood straight facing John. As John paused, gathering his thoughts, Max spoke for the first time since the greeting as he had entered the office.

"I've let you down, John. I've suffered every day. All day every day. When she told me she was with child, I lost my mind. I was going to kill myself. I was going to take her and run. I didn't know what to do. I've always tried to do the right thing, but I didn't know if there was a right thing. I cannot forgive myself and I don't expect you to forgive me. I'll do whatever you ask. Hang me at daybreak. Tell me to leave, and I'll be out of here before the sun comes up. I can't make it right, John. I'm sorry and ashamed, and I can't even ask how I can make it right. There ain't no way I know that could ever make it right."

He spoke quietly and tears ran down his face, not in fear because he had no fear of anything that John might do, but in abject sorrow for what he had done. John leaned forward and placed his elbows on the desk, resting his face in his hands. He sat without speaking for more than a minute. That minute seemed an eternity to Max.

He raised his head up, and there were tears in John's eyes as well. "Max, I've had so much on my mind. You can't believe how much there is to starting a business like the railroad. I want to think on this, and I'll talk to you later. I'd like for you to go back to the range shack and stay until I've had some time. I don't want to make a decision now that I'll regret later. You know I'm disappointed and hurt, but it ain't ever good to make a decision in this frame of mind. Just go take care of things on the range, and I'll send for you later. I don't know how long it will be. Somehow I have to get through this party, then I just don't know. Maybe a couple of days or maybe a week."

"Yes, sir," Max said as he started to turn. He hesitated and turned back: "John, you do whatever you think's right, and I'll do whatever you say." Then he turned and left, returning to his horse.

It had not been more than fifteen minutes since he had entered the house. Riding through the darkness, he arrived at the range shack just as the sky was starting to get light over the Gulf of Mexico.

Unable to think of sleeping, he had breakfast in the kitchen and changed horses for the day's work on the range. There were new calves to be looked after, fences to repair, horses to groom and shoe, wood to cut, and all the chores necessary to run a cattle operation.

* * * *

The cowboys were good enough that even though they talked among themselves, none asked Max what had transpired. Their only words to him were concerning the work to be done. They were all well aware that he was the man in charge, and at the moment, that had not changed.

At one point in the afternoon Max was headed for the corral to cut out a fresh mount, planning to work until dark. As he passed two cowboys holding a young calf down, one of the men looked up and laughed. Max, on edge all day, knew the men were aware of what was going on. Such things are never really secret.

He stopped, walked over to the grinning cowboy, and prepared to hit him for his insolence. "What's so funny, Luke?" Luke blanched, seeing the fire in Max's eyes. "It's this steer, Max. He got in some cactus, and he's got some stickers in his pecker. We can't get his pecker out of his belly so we can pull the stickers out. He runs it out when we ain't tryin' to pull the stickers, but soon as we try to pull one, he jerks it back in. We're havin' a hell of a time." Max left them to the steer's predicament, relieved and a little embarrassed for having thought the man had been laughing at his predicament.

Time passed and Max worked to exhaustion each day in order to be able to sleep some at night. It was four days before John sent a rider to ask Max to return to the house. His mind was in turmoil as he rode, leaving his mount to choose the gait. He was dreading the meeting with John, and at the same time he had a feeling of relief that soon he would know his fate.

John was somber as Max entered the office. Again, John sat behind the desk and Max judged this was not to be a friendly chat. John indicated the chair in front of the desk, and Max sat down, upright and looking directly at John. He did not speak, waiting for John to talk.

"Max, I have sent Charlene away. That part of my life is past." There was a long pause as John chose his words carefully. "You and I have been together since the war, and I can't recall a cross word between us during that time. I know you to be an honorable man. You've been loyal to a fault and as good a friend as a man could ask for. I know in my mind that you were not to blame for what has happened.

"As I said, I've known from the first day I met Charlene that she was possessed by the devil. She has a raging desire she cannot control. When she is under the spell of the devil, she will not take no for an answer. I truly believe you could not have resisted her."

Max looked down then, unable to look John in the eye. "John," he said without looking up, "I knew what I was doing was wrong. I knew it at the time, but I just could not stop. It was so wrong, but I was out of control. I, too, was possessed by the devil. That ain't no excuse. I ain't makin' no excuse, and whatever you want me to do, I'll do. Ain't no way I can ever make it right."

With that, the two men sat quietly on the subject for some time. John had spent much time thinking while Max was away tending to work. The burden of the business demanded his attention. He desperately needed Max to run things at the ranch, and it would be almost impossible to find anyone as capable and trustworthy as Max to take his place. And there was the boy, Little John. The boy needed someone to look up to and teach him. John could not be there for the boy and spend the time away necessary to conduct the other business.

"There is no need for you to leave, Max," John said. "You're a good man, and I'd never be able to trust another man as I trust you. You've violated that trust, and it's hard for both of us. You've learned from that, and we both know how you regret it. I need you here. I need you to be a teacher for my son. It's too far for him to go to town to school, so he'll need someone to teach him reading, writing, and numbers. There ain't no one better to teach him how to be a man. I'm askin' you to stay. Look after the ranch and take care of my boy. I'll be gone even more than I have been. We'll talk no more of that woman, and I don't want you to ever talk about her again. All anyone needs to know is that she's gone."

And that was all that was said about the infidelity with Charlene. The talk continued about other topics: problems on the ranch and how the railroad was making good progress and would have usable track within the year. The first land grants were due soon, and sale of some of those lands would provide additional financing.

CHAPTER
XI

It would be almost a year before freight transportation and passenger travel would become profitable. The railroad company's board of directors worked well together, and John had the same thoughts as Joseph Telfner. Hiring started almost immediately and word spread throughout East Texas that the railroad was hiring.

Men came from miles away to sign up to construct the rail line. The surveyors were at work laying out the route with earth-moving crews following to level the roadbed, fill gullies, provide drainage, and blast outcroppings of rock—all necessary for preparing the land for rails.

John spent long hours in his new office checking every detail of the business, and it became his responsibility to replace unreliable or incompetent men at every level below the owners of the line. His work was all consuming, and he had little thought of the ranch or his son.

Max was fully capable of running the ranch and seeing after the rearing of John's son. The boy was unusually attentive and learned quickly. Tutors were brought in to teach young John his numbers, reading, writing, and history. A normal day required the young man to spend three to four hours in intensive study, with the time usually divided between two tutors. The remainder of the day was spent with the hired hands, assisting them in conducting the actual running of the ranch.

Several of the cowboys Little John worked with were from Mexico, and the boy learned their language as well as he knew English. By the age of five he was completely fluent in Spanish. More accurately, he learned "Mexican," since there were many differences in the Spanish spoken by native Spanish families and the guttural Mexican language spoken by these cowboys. Their language was liberally spiced with words and expressions from the native Indians and indigenous people of Mexico as well as Anglo words and expressions they had adopted.

Max and Little John spent hours practicing with the firearms in common use. Max enjoyed the feel of fine weapons and the accuracy inherent in fine firearms. There was probably no better teacher, since Max not only was unusually capable in the use of weapons, he also enjoyed the competition of shooting with other marksmen.

It was rare for him to lose a match with any weapon—hand gun, long gun, or knife. His fast draw was unbelievable; he could draw from his holster, fire six rounds at a line of empty bottles, and replace the gun in its holster before the glass from the bottles fell to the ground. And there was seldom a bottle left standing unscathed.

Little John was given a .22 Winchester rifle for his seventh birthday. It was a single-shot, single-action rifle that would fire any of the .22 caliber shells. It was not the first exposure John had to firearms, as he'd been raised with the cowboys who almost always carried more than one weapon.

Max lined up six empty cans from the kitchen and let Little John practice with the new gun. He did surprisingly well, and on his first try hit four of the six cans from a distance of about twenty yards. "Good shooting," Max exclaimed. "You're a natural." With that, Max drew his own pistol and popped the two remaining cans from the fence rail.

During those years, Max permitted the cowboys to bring their families to live in the ranch-hand quarters. They were comfortable, and each cowboy with a wife or family had a small private room to themselves. The children were free to play, and Little John spent much of his youth playing with the Mexican children, as there were no other children of his age on the ranch.

It was a rough and tumble life, and the boys spent much of their time in competitive sports: wrestling, throwing rocks, shooting small-caliber weapons, and demonstrating their skill as horsemen. All were capable of riding, roping, and all manner of horsemanship by the time they were nine or ten.

Max watched the boys, and when they were capable of riding with the adults, he put them on the payroll to work with the men. Some as young as twelve had a starting salary of fifty cents then worked their way up to as much as three dollars a month. It was a proud moment, a move into manhood, for the young men when they were selected to ride the range for wages.

Little John rode with the cowboys, and when he was nine was permitted to spend nights with the cowboys on the range. He loved the life and by fifteen was as good at the craft as the best of them. The spring months when the cattle were rounded up for branding, sorting, and neutering were his favorite days on the open range. There were times when he did not return to the main house for four or five days, living on the range with the crew he chose to work with.

The men continued the old tradition of an afternoon siesta and napped for thirty minutes to an hour after a lunch of beans and cornbread. Many of the cowboys preferred to roll their beans in a tamale, but John, as he was now known, preferred the cornbread, with a large slice of onion and beans.

Work was usually finished by late afternoon and the men were free to relax and sit around the mesquite campfire. Usually there was a bottle of tequila passed around, but John never accepted the offer of a sip from the bottle. Instead, he would go alone to shoot his pistol, using the disposed-of cans and bottles from the chuck wagon as targets.

The younger cowboys would join him, and frequently they had a contest to see who the best shot was and who could draw, fire, hit the target, and return his pistol to his holster fastest. John was so proficient he seldom lost a contest.

The young men could not afford the cost of ammunition, but Max was always liberal in providing John with whatever shells he required and often had a new weapon for him to try. His favorite was a .32 caliber Smith & Wesson revolver.

With the help of a daughter of one of the head wranglers, John also became a man. It was one very pleasant evening when John was alone by the small stream below the bunkhouse. The girl joined him there, and small talk progressed to her holding his hand and, after a time, offering a kiss. Shortly after, the kiss aroused passion in the young man, and he found no resistance as he possessed the young girl.

The affair lasted through the spring of that year but cooled during the summer as they both found other interests. They remained on friendly terms and joined in the usual activities at the ranch, but the girl married an older man that fall, one of the vaqueros working on the ranch.

With the large land holdings, it became necessary to hire additional cowboys to manage the land and look after the cattle. Fencing, which had been almost nonexistent when John Welder first bought the land, was becoming necessary. Fence building and repairs became an important part of ranching.

By the time young John turned nineteen, Max asked whether he would like to go to the border and hire fifteen to twenty Mexican cowboys. John had gone in the past with Max and one of the foremen to hire vaqueros. He felt confident that he could handle the job.

With Cisero Toda and another young cowboy named José, John set out on horseback for the Mexican border. They rode with a small remuda of three saddle horses and two pack mules for provisions.

Chapter
XII

Three riders made their way west through the tall grass, mesquite trees, and occasional patch of prickly pear cactus.

The rider in the lead was Ham Caine, a handsome man of thirty years or so. He was well dressed, riding a chestnut mare that responded easily to the guidance of the rider. Some yards behind, the second rider, Snake Alvarez, didn't seem to bother to guide his horse. The horse simply followed the leader with little or no direction from its rider.

Snake Alvarez was a swarthy man in his mid-thirties, half gringo and half Hispanic. His mother was a Mexican prostitute who was impregnated by a cowboy from Texas who had crossed the border for a night of drinking and whoring. His offspring never knew him nor even heard his name. Alvarez was the family name of his mother.

At twelve, Snake had left his home in Mexico and crossed the border for a better life in Texas. Working as a ranch hand any place he could find; he had become a proficient horseman and better than all the other cowboys with a handgun. The gun seemed a part of him and he was as fast as anyone he knew in drawing the weapon from his holster and firing. His accuracy was exceptional, and he had killed many rattlers from the saddle while riding the range.

The third rider didn't seem to be with the two others. He was well back, five hundred yards or more, following but not with them. The trio rode west for another three hours and came upon a small stream with running water. Ham, the obvious leader, stopped to let his mount drink from the stream. He looked around and, even though it was not late, he decided to camp there for the night.

As the straggling boy rode up, Ham explained it could well be the last good location to spend the night and told him to gather wood and build a campfire. He suggested to Snake that a rabbit or two cooked over the fire would make a good evening meal. The three made camp, sat around the fire until well after dark, then settled in for the night.

During the night, Snake woke up to relieve himself then walked over to check the horses at their tether. Noticing the horse droppings, he decided to play a prank on the boy. He quietly retrieved one of the boy's boots and placed a choice horse turd in the boot. Using a small stick, he worked it into the toe of the boot.

Replacing the boot, he settled in to await the morning. Ham was the first to awaken, but Snake, being a light sleeper, opened his eyes at the first sound of movement by Ham. The boy still slept peacefully with his feet exposed below the horse blanket he used for cover. Snake kicked the boy's foot. "Get up and get some more wood so we can make some coffee," he commanded.

Knowing from experience that nothing would be gained by ignoring the command, the boy threw off the horse blanket and reached for his boots. He had slept in his clothes, so he only needed to slip on his boots and strap on his gun. Still sitting, he pulled one boot on and started on the second boot when he realized something was wrong. Something was in the boot. The horse shit had squeezed between his toes by the time he realized he had been the victim of a nasty prank.

His anger flared and he cursed his partners. He threw his gun belt around his waist, quickly buckled it, and adjusted the holster. "Touch that gun, boy, and I'll kill you." The laughter died and Snake adjusted his stance, ready to draw should the boy continue on his path. Ham pressed the trigger on his own pistol, concealed below the rough blanket, and silently cocked the weapon. He would end the fight, if necessary, by shooting Snake to save the boy's life.

The boy shook with rage, but his fear of Snake overcame his anger and he backed down. Tears spilling from his eyes only added humiliation to his defeat. He cleaned the boot as best he could and went to gather wood for the fire.

The trio continued west after a cup of hot coffee and some hard biscuits moistened by the coffee. In a short time, they saw the bell tower of a church and thought they had arrived at their destination, the village of Harlingen. As they entered the village, they realized it was not Harlingen but a few houses built around an old Spanish mission. It was a place called San Benito.

At the first house, a young Mexican girl sat on a platform made of stone that surrounded a rusted water pump. A younger girl was washing her hair, pumping water from the well as needed to wash her friend's hair. Bonita, the girl with wet hair, was stripped to her waist, with budding breasts that captured the gaze of the three riders. "Jesus," breathed the boy as he eyed the girl. "That is sure some sweet meat!"

Water from the well ran down from the landing into a small tank, and the three riders permitted the horses to drink from the tank. As the three riders dismounted, the younger girl was frightened by their appearance and ran from the yard. Bonita, eyes closed to avoid the soapy water, heard the approach of the horses but was unaware of the presence of the three riders. Reaching up for the pump handle, she pumped water to rinse her own hair. That movement totally revealed her bare breasts, and Ham reached for her wrist on the pump handle.

Bonita's father rose from the old chair and spoke to the men. "Please, señors. She is only a child. You'll scare her." Lupita, the younger girl, watched from the safety of a patch of Johnson grass outside the yard. "Don't worry, old man," Ham said. "We're not going to hurt your daughter. Just having a little fun." He pulled the girl from her sitting position and drew her to him. "Yer' a cute lil' bitch," Ham said as he held her close to his chest with an arm around her.

Fear welled up inside her father, and the old man pleaded, saying again, "Please, señor. She's only a child. Please don't frighten her like that." Ignoring his plea, Ham started toward the house, pulling the girl along by her wrist. Without giving it a thought, her father reached for the old single-shot twelve-gauge leaning against the wall near where he had been sitting, hoping to dissuade the man from molesting his daughter.

Snake, striking like his nickname, shot the man before he could raise the old gun and threaten them with it. At the sound of the shot, the girl's mother rushed from the house. There, mortally wounded and lying on the ground was her husband, and she bent over him. "Torino! Torino!" she cried. "What have you done?" She fell to her knees and gathered her husband in her arms.

———◦◦◦———

Chapter
XIII

Young John and his crew of two camped outside Corpus Christi the first night and spent the next two days traveling to the Rio Grande Valley, arriving at the small village of San Benito late afternoon of the third day. The two vaqueros stayed with the horses at the livery, and John spent the night at the home of a widow, Mrs. Johnson. He had been there before with Max so he knew the widow, who welcomed him with open arms.

It was good to spend the night in a real bed, and after a good night's sleep, John was up and ready to attend to the business of hiring cowboys. Word quickly spread on their arrival that a man from the Welder Ranch was in town and hiring men to work.

John had a hearty breakfast of five eggs, fried potatoes, and biscuits and gravy. As he ate, another man entered the kitchen, looked at John, and spoke to Mrs. Johnson. "I'll have what he's having," he said, and extended his hand to John. "My name's Lester Caine. I'm the deputy sheriff from Harlingen. Had word that someone had been hung down here by the river."

He joined John at the table and continued, "Some cowboys caught three meskins driving cattle toward the river and strung them up to a big oak tree. They spooked the horses, and the mounts headed home across the river. The kinfolk will be by after dark to get the bodies. Take them home for burial. Nothing else I need to do."

The deputy ate fast between his words and finished the meal before John. "I'll go by on my way back home and see if their folks got the bodies yet," he said. "With the fightin' down there, we been havin' more and more raids by them poor bastards. Been a lawman here in the valley for twenty years. Most of the trouble we see is the meskins coming across to steal livestock or anything else that ain't locked up."

He wiped his mouth on his sleeve before continuing, "I've shot some, but usually they scramble and head back to the river before I can catch up. Been in a tight spot more than once when they wanted to stay and fight. Been shot twice but nothin' serious. Got me in the leg once and that took a couple of months to heal."

As he was speaking, a young Mexican girl rushed into the house through the back door. "Help me," Lupita screamed in Spanish. "They are killing the Credos!" John pushed back from the table, but the deputy remained seated. "Don't worry about that, son. Them meskins are always fighting. I'll sort it out later if it comes to anything. Sit and have another cup of coffee. Mrs. Johnson is sure one fine cook, and she makes the best coffee north of the Rio Grande."

The child, frantic to get help for her friends, tugged at John's sleeve. "Please, señor!" she begged in English. "Banditos! Banditos! Gringo banditos. They shoot Señor Credo!"

John rushed to his room where his gun belt lay on top of his saddlebags. He quickly strapped the gun belt on and tied the leather strap to his thigh. "I'll go along, but I doubt it's anything to get excited about." Caine was still reluctant to become involved, but he strapped on his own weapon and left the house behind John, who walked so rapidly the deputy had difficulty keeping up.

Chapter
XIV

As she held Torino tight to her breast, Bonita's mother saw the two gringos coming down the dusty path toward the house. The two outlaws in the yard noticed the men as well and turned to confront them. The taller of the two men was a few steps ahead of the older man as they approached. "What's going on here?" he asked.

"None of your business, stranger. Better just turn around and head back to where you came from." Snake touched the butt of his holstered gun but did not draw.

"Little girl said there was trouble. Someone got shot?" John asked.

"Por favor," pleaded the Mexican woman. "The other bandito has my daughter inside. Save her!"

John stepped toward the house as the deputy held back, not sure about facing the two armed men in the yard. Snake made his move and started to draw, while the boy, trying to follow his lead, fumbled for his own gun. John drew, fired twice at Snake, then shot the boy in the face, killing him instantly. He fired once more, striking Snake in the forehead.

The mother grabbed a hayfork lying nearby and dashed into the house, determined to save her child from the leader of the gang. Too late, for Ham, in his lust, had completed the act and lay naked on the bed, his gun belt on a small stand beside the bed.

Hearing the gunfire outside, Ham reached for the weapon as the mother entered the room. He saw her lunge with the hayfork and shot her through the chest. The hayfork pierced his side as the mother fell dead beside the bed. "Son of a bitch," he cried. Grasping the handle, he easily pulled a tine from his side, as it had only pierced the skin, leaving both an entry and exit wound but doing little real damage.

Hearing more gunfire, he leapt naked from the window of the bedroom into the side yard, crouching low with his pistol in hand. He moved cautiously toward the rear of the house. Bonita quickly pulled her dress over her naked body and ran toward the front door.

"He's outside," she shouted in Spanish. "He's gone that way," pointing to her left toward the side of the house. John, gun in hand, started toward the corner of the house, carefully looking around the side. As John's hat appeared from behind the house, Ham fired, scattering some wood chips harmlessly.

Moving swiftly, John left the safety of the house for a clear shot at the bandit. His first shot hit Ham in the gun arm above the elbow, shattering the arm. The gun fell from his useless hand, and he reached for it with his left hand. The next shot from John's gun tore through Ham's left leg with consequences similar to the shot that had destroyed his arm. Ham fell back, stunned and beaten, his gun out of reach and no options left.

"You've got me, stranger. Do it! Finish it!" He did not cower or beg. "Just finish it, you son of a bitch," he yelled.

"No, I'll not kill you, you sorry excuse for a man," John said, speaking in a normal voice but clearly intending to be intimidating. "You're gonna live long enough to regret what you've done, and you're going to root in that cow shit to show what a pig you are." John indicated a fresh pile of cow manure the family milk cow had deposited at the edge of the yard.

"Go to hell. Just finish me and be done with it."

"Do what I said, or my next shot is going to take off your cods," John replied as he took careful aim at the exposed genitals of the man on the ground.

His left leg now useless, Ham tried to cover himself with his right leg and left hand but was unable to do so. Facing death was something he was capable of, but the thought of losing his manhood terrified him. He rolled to his left, cringing as the shattered leg bore the weight of his body, and he pulled himself toward the cow manure only a few feet away.

Gently, he nudged the pile with his nose. "That ain't gonna' do," John said. "Root like a pig and grunt." John was now standing just a few feet behind the outlaw, whose testicles were fully exposed.

It had not happened since he was a young boy, but tears welled in his eyes and Ham cried in shame and embarrassment. He began to grunt loudly as he pushed his face into the fresh manure. The girl he had just deflowered came to his side, spat on his back, and placed a bare foot on his head, pushing him deeper into the fresh manure.

"Pig! Goddamn, gringo pig," she sneered as she abused him. There was no hint of sympathy or remorse as she ground his face into the manure. Crying herself now, she rushed back to the house and the fallen bodies of her dead parents.

Turning to the deputy, John spoke matter-of-factly. "He'll be dead in a couple of hours. Let him suffer that long. He deserves all he gets."

The deputy went to check on the bloody man. "Christ!" he said. "That's Ham Caine! He's my cousin. We had the same grandpa. Haven't seen him in six or eight years, but that's sure as hell him." He stared a little longer. "I'll let his folks know."

CHAPTER
XV

As John and the deputy started back to the rooming house, the priest from the old Spanish mission in San Benito arrived. He went to the prostrate outlaw and saw the pitiful condition of the man on the ground. Rolling him on his back, he started cleaning the manure from his face and chest.

Praying silently, Father Diego went for a rag hanging on a nearby clothesline and used the rag to clean the man as best he could. By then, there were half a dozen neighbors in the yard, curious to see what the gunshots had been about. The priest asked if someone would help carry the wounded man to the mission so he could die in peace under the watchful eye of God. Most were reluctant to do anything for the gringo, but the obligation to their parish priest eventually overcame their hesitation.

Using the plank door to the goat shed as a stretcher, they carried the body the short distance to the mission, entered the dark rectory, placed him on the bed where the priest normally slept, and quickly left. Kneeling beside the bed, Father Diego administered the last rites of the church before continuing to clean the body. He had no hope that the bandit would live but felt deeply he should be clean to face God at his judgment.

Now unconscious, Ham lay motionless as the priest ministered to his wounds as best he could. The bone in the arm was shattered and small bits of bone protruded. Removing what fragments he could see, the priest cleaned the wounds and poured kerosene on them from the can he kept for the lamp. Going to the dark storeroom, he gathered all the spider webs he could find and returned and covered both open wounds with the webbing he had gathered. He bandaged the arm and leg with strips of white cloth from a sheet.

As there was nothing more he could do for the dying man, Father Diego knelt by the bedside and continued praying for his soul. Expecting the man to die during the afternoon, the priest took his usual siesta and checked for signs of life when he awoke. The bandit still lived but was comatose.

The priest raised the limp man's head and attempted to give him a sip of water. For his trouble, he was rewarded with a slight cough as the water entered Ham's windpipe. After evening mass, attended by more than the usual number of faithful who were still curious about the wounded bandit, Father Diego once more checked Ham's condition.

Still breathing in short gasps, the bandit lived. After midnight the exhausted priest slept in brief, fitful naps until daylight. The bandit still showed signs of life. There was nothing more to do, so the priest covered the wounded man with a sheet and went about his daily routine of morning prayers then Mass followed by breakfast of cold gruel and a piece of bread. As he worked during the day, he checked frequently to see whether the man had died.

At the end of the second full day in the priest's care, the man made a small noise. A groan or so it seemed. Perhaps, just perhaps, he would live. The second night was much the same as the first, with the bandit only barely alive and showing little sign of any hope for survival.

The third day Father Diego carefully removed the bandage from the man's arm. The wound was open and raw. He washed it again with kerosene and searched for more spider webs. The bandages were blood soaked, but the bleeding had slowed to nothing more than seepage. He replaced the blood-soaked bandage with fresh cloth, repeating the procedure with the wounded leg.

Late that morning in the priest's bed, the bandit again made a noise, and when the priest checked him, the bandit's eyelids fluttered. Father Diego fell to his knees to thank God. After praying, he brought a cup of water, raised the man's head, and tried with a spoon to give him water. He swallowed! Clearly, he had taken a sip of water.

The careful ministrations lasted for more than a week before the bandit opened his eyes. There were no words, no indication the bandit was in pain or even knew where he was. His eyes were open but did not focus on anything.

The priest's first attempt at giving Ham nourishment was as unsuccessful as the first attempt to give him water. The man would not swallow. It was almost two weeks before Ham first swallowed a small spoon of corn grits, then he mumbled something Father Diego could not understand. He watched the eyes carefully, and it seemed the bandit focused his eyes and looked at the priest's face, only inches from his own. His lips moved, but there were no words.

For the next week, Ham took both water and small sips of soup the priest had made. And so it went, for weeks before the man was able to respond to questions from the priest. No one else had been in to see the man. The deputy sheriff did not realize the man had survived, and the local parishioners had lost interest in the welfare of the bandit.

Care for the bandit became a routine part of his daily chores for Father Diego. He changed the bedclothes as they became soiled and cleaned the man with a washcloth and pan of water. After four months, Ham had recovered enough to be able to speak, haltingly at first, but becoming stronger day by day.

Seven months following the gunfight with the tall Texan, Ham was able to sit upright, propped up by pillows at the head of the bed. After eight months, he was able to swing his legs off the bed and sit with the help of the priest. He could put no weight on his left leg nor use his right arm at all. The fingers would move, but the upper arm was not connected by bone. Only the skin, sinew, and muscle connected the arm where the ball from the Texan's gun had shattered the bone.

Moving the arm sent excruciating flashes of pain through his body, so Father Diego fashioned a sling from two pieces of rag to immobilize the arm across Ham's abdomen.

Chapter
XVI

The Bank Robbery

The three days following the gunfight, John talked to fifty or sixty men and boys looking for work at the Welder Ranch. Having grown to manhood in the company of vaqueros, John was familiar with the qualities he admired in a good cowboy.

At the end of the questioning, he had hired fifteen men. The youngest was a fifteen-year-old boy who demonstrated more than average knowledge regarding ranching and horsemanship. He was well dressed, polite, and spoke a few words of English.

Another one was an older vaquero who had worked in Texas before but had returned to Mexico to care for family and now was ready to go back to work in the States. He was fluent in both English and Spanish, with only a slight accent when speaking in English. Both would be useful since the men at the various locations were a mix of Anglo and Mexican wranglers.

John, fluent in both languages, was in no need of a translator. Half the men were riding horses, and John bought enough horses and saddles from a local ranch for the rest. The horses were of good stock, but the saddles were discards, well-worn and in need of repair. Quickly John had them repaired and suitable for the trip.

They traveled north, and John made camp for the night outside a town named Alice. After a night under the stars, John sent the men on with Cisero in charge. He rode into Alice with José, the young man he had brought from home, and with the pack mule to replenish supplies for the long trip home. As they arrived in town, the store had just opened for the day and John started selecting the things needed for the trip.

Just as the store owner started adding up the bill, there was a commotion outside with gunfire. Rushing outside to see what was happening, John saw a young man across the street at the side of the local bank, holding two horses. As he watched, an older man ran from the bank carrying two bags. The bags were strapped together much as saddlebags, and the bandit quickly tied the bags behind the saddle and mounted the horse.

This was clearly a bank robbery in progress. John drew his pistol and fired at the man, now mounted and turning toward the open country behind the bank. The younger man, unable to mount his frightened horse, drew his pistol and fired across the street toward John. In a panic and in fear of his life, the boy decided to drop his gun and raised his hands.

John shot him and mounted his horse, tethered there in front of the store. Riding to overtake the robber, he caught up after a chase of more than half a mile. He shot the man from his saddle, and the horse ran a short distance before stopping, finally realizing he no longer had a rider.

John easily retrieved the horse and returned with it to the fallen robber. Lifting the lifeless body, he placed it across the saddle, lashed it in place, and took the dead robber back to Alice. By the time he returned, there was a crowd of people in the street, talking loudly about the attempt to rob the bank.

The shot John had first heard had been from inside the bank. The man he had just killed had shot the teller but not fatally. The man had only a painful wound between his left shoulder and upper chest. Two men were working on the fallen banker and had sent for the local doctor, a veterinarian, who lived a short distance outside the town.

An older man confronted John, demanding, "Why did you shoot that boy? He had thrown down his gun and had his hands raised!" John, having had enough excitement for one morning, explained, "I couldn't spend time holding him and have any chance of catching the other one. No one had the gumption to even offer a hand. You'd rather I let him ride off?" The man was not satisfied with the answer but saw the anger in John's face so did not press the matter.

By the time the doctor arrived to care for the fallen bank clerk, the deputy sheriff had arrived. John explained what had transpired, and the deputy was satisfied with the outcome. He shook hands with John and thanked him for the way he had taken charge of the situation.

"Just glad you were here. I don't think any of the locals could have handled it," he said.

John finished his business in the store and loaded the pack mule. He and José rode north to catch up with the group of newly hired men. The remainder of the trip to the Welder ranch was without incident, but by the time John arrived home, the word had spread throughout South Texas that young John Welder had killed five bandits in the same week.

When Governor Davis read the account of Welder's exploits, he called the captain of the Rangers in Austin. "You see that story about Welder down in South Texas?" he asked. "See if you can get that boy into the Rangers. That's the kind of man we need. You got anybody down around Victoria that can talk to him?"

"I've seen the stories, Governor," said the captain. "I know his dad. His dad has offices here in Austin. I'll talk to him, but I doubt the boy would be interested. He's got more than he can handle with the Welder land holdings. The Welders have gathered up one of the biggest spreads in Texas."

"Christ! I didn't even make the connection! I didn't know that was John Welder's boy," the governor exclaimed. "I've known John for years. I'll talk to him myself. You go talk to the boy, and I'll talk to his dad. I saw the name, but thought it was just a coincidence, two people with the same name."

Young John was closer to Max Stone than with his dad. The two had been together far more than John and his dad. Max had once thought of becoming a lawman himself following the war. He encouraged young John to follow his heart and do what he wanted to do, not what he felt responsible to do. The ranch would be in good hands without him. Max knew the boy, and he could see that although he was doing an excellent job, he did not really have his heart in ranching.

Chapter
XVII

In just two years, John was accepted into the Texas Rangers, having completed all requirements and tests with outstanding results. His first assignment following graduation was with the Capitol Police at the Governor's Office in Austin. His primary duties were the protection of the governor and security of the state capitol.

It was interesting work, but it was almost entirely routine security services with little criminal activity involved. He longed to be in the field working real criminal cases and searching for wanted or dangerous felons.

Having a much better education than the other officers in the detail and paying such diligent attention to his duties, he soon received an outstanding letter of recommendation to the commander of the Rangers. His next assignment was to the Southern District, which covered all of the Rio Grande Valley as far west as Del Rio.

The Mexican raiders, working as supporters of the Mexican revolutionary, Pancho Villa, were constantly making incursions across the Rio Grande to replenish supplies no longer available at any price in Mexico. Coming upon a group of eight men with four pack horses in tow, John confronted the men. The pack horses were loaded with supplies both bought and stolen, and the group was headed south toward the Rio Grande.

John spoke to the obvious leader of the group. "I'll need to check the horses," he said in Spanish. As he spoke to the leader, six of the men rode up to sit aside their leader, three on each side. One rider remained at the rear of the line of pack horses, binding each horse to the one ahead with a lead line.

"With great respect, I must refuse, señor," the man replied. "I have far to go and no time to allow an inspection." The men beside their leader sat erect in their saddles with obvious resolve to support their leader in whatever choice he made.

"I'm a Texas Ranger, señor," John said. There was no English used as they conversed only in Spanish. "I must insist. Take your men, ride a hundred meters down the trail, and wait while I inspect your horses."

There was a brief silence while the leader of the group considered his options. Clearly, he could not allow an inspection, since much of the cargo was stolen goods—primarily guns and ammunition.

"I regret that I must refuse, señor. If you will move aside, I will continue on my journey." His hand touched the butt of his pistol as he spoke. Following his lead, the others, except for the two that held long guns, moved their hands toward sidearms.

John spurred his horse as he drew his weapon. None expected the sudden charge of the horse, and they were distracted as the horse surged forward the ten feet or so toward their leader. John shot the leader from his saddle before any were able to react. As he passed the leader's horse, he shot the man to his right.

With the unexpected rush by the ranger and the noise of the gunshots, the horses went into full panic. Unable to control their mounts and shoot at the same time, the remaining men were helpless as John wheeled his horse around and shot two more of the Mexicans.

In the confusion one horse reared, and the man lost his seat on the horse as it fell to the side. John shot him before he could recover from the fall. The two remaining riders spurred their panicked horses and attempted to escape the crazy ranger. The final man behind the pack horses abandoned his post and followed the two fleeing men.

John pulled the Sharps repeating rifle from the saddle scabbard and shot the man who had been guarding the rear. The two remaining bandits were too far for a clear shot and riding as hard as they could to escape with their lives.

John spent the remainder of the day removing saddles and bridles from the dead men's horses, leaving the horses to make their own way home or go free. Leaving the bodies where they lay, he returned to San Antonio with the pack horses, where he turned them over to the local sheriff.

Notified of a shooting in Victoria via telegraph, he took the train to check on the event. It was clearly in the jurisdiction of local law enforcement but of interest to the Rangers because several people were involved. A racial disturbance of some sort had erupted when a group of white men entered the black neighborhood on East Juan

Linn Street. A lynch mob was intent on finding a black man who had been accused of molesting a white woman near the Guadalupe River.

John's train arrived at the station after midnight, not far from the site of the reported incident. Too late to do anything, John retrieved his horse from the cattle car and rode the short distance to the livery stable on Commercial Street. Without rousing the owner of the livery, he stabled the horse and removed the saddle and bridle. He took a scoop of crushed grain for the horse and checked the water trough.

With the horse cared for, he walked the short distance down the same street to the white house that had a red lantern hanging over the front steps. There was a light inside, and he could hear voices. Knocking on the door, he was greeted by a nice-looking lady in evening clothes—a nightgown of sorts with a very low neckline.

Two ladies of the evening sat at the kitchen table with two very drunk middle-age men. "Come in, cowboy," the madam said. "You're out late and you've just about missed the party." She opened the door wide for him to enter and held out her hand.

"I'm Sally and people call me Sally Ride. The girls are busy, but if you care to come on in, I can help you with anything you need. Whiskey? Locoweed? Anything you would like that the law allows."

He took her hand. "Thanks, ma'am, friendly of you. I been up longer than I like and need a good night's rest. You got an empty bed I could get?" With a welcoming grin and a demure look, she responded, "You betcha, cowboy. I got a bed for a dollar and you can have someone keep you warm for a couple of dollars more."

John was not surprised and suddenly not as tired as when he had left the livery stable. "That's very neighborly of you, ma'am," he said. "I ain't used to such a welcome, but I'll sure take you up on the warm bed."

The party at the kitchen table paid little attention as she started up the stairs to a bedroom with the ranger in tow. As the pair stripped and got into bed, there was little conversation before they became intimate. The mating was intense and Sally, as she almost always did, enjoyed the ride.

Both fell into an exhausted sleep and did not awaken until the sunlight burst into the room through an open window. Sally turned to the young man, kissing him gently on the cheek to stir him from a deep sleep. Confused at first, he thought back to the night before. *Wow!* he thought, *that was a short night.*

They were covered only by a sheet, and he raised it to reveal her beautiful and totally nude body beside him. "Your rent's all paid up, cowboy," she said, as she stroked his cheek and kissed him gently on the lips. "You feel like it, you can have another go."

John was only too happy to agree and once more indulged in the lust that consumed them both. "Jesus!" she said. "You are one bareback rider that can't be throwed."

He smiled at the compliment and said, "You are just one wild mare I didn't want to get off of. I learned to ride when I was just a kid. A nice meskin gal taught me how when I was just fourteen. I rode with the vaqueros, and I was full grown by the time I was fifteen. Max taught me most of what I know. He's my uncle."

Sally choked, gasped, and had trouble breathing for a minute. Can't be! God, don't let it be, she thought. "Your Uncle Max?" she asked. "He your mom's brother or your dad's brother?"

"Oh no. I just always call him Uncle Max 'cause he is just like an uncle. Actually, he was the honcho at the ranch. Came south with my dad after the war."

Sally turned away to hide the tears. She could not let him know. *I've slept with my own son! My God! What have I done?* John got up from the bed when she turned away and went to the water closet to relieve himself." I need to get going and see about that problem over on the other side of the tracks," he said.

He washed his face and hands, then dressed, leaned across the bed, and kissed Sally on the cheek. She did not respond and did not turn to face him. As he descended the stairs, he overheard girls talking in the kitchen. "Good morning, girls," he said.

They both looked his way with large grins. "Come sit and have some coffee, cowboy," one of the whores said. "Have some breakfast if you like. Minny Bell's a good cook and she can fix anything you like."

Minny Bell was a small Negro woman, not more than four feet tall. She had been working for Mrs. Ride since she was first starting in business.

She cared for—and pampered—Sally's daughter as if she were her own child.

Patty had her own room in the back of the house and was not permitted upstairs at night, but she had the run of the rest of the house. In the evenings, she always went to her own room. It was always that way and she thought nothing of it. There was never any secret regarding the way her mother supported herself and the girls who worked for her mom. The girls came and went, and none stayed more than a couple of years. Some stayed only a few weeks, until they could accumulate enough money to move on. Some were as young as sixteen and a few as old as sixty. The older men often chose the older women, being embarrassed to be with the much younger girls.

Minny cooked John a good breakfast of eggs and pork chops with milk gravy and hot buttermilk biscuits. "Thanks, girls. I feel like I could wrestle a grizzly bear now." He took two silver dollars from his pants pocket and left them on the table.

"That's one for Minny for a good breakfast, and one for you girls for being good company." Leaving the house, he retrieved his horse from the livery stable next door and paid the proprietor for his service and feed for the horse.

By the time he had concluded his business, the stable boy had the horse saddled and ready to ride. The horse was shiny as a new dime with a complete grooming by the stable boy, combed down with the currycomb and oiled hooves even. John retrieved a quarter from his pocket and gave it to the boy. The boy said, "You're a Texas Ranger, ain'tcha? You ain't got no call to tip me, sir. I'm just proud to be the one cared for your mount. Fine animal!" The boy pocketed the quarter, however, with no offer to return it. "You come back any time and ask for me. I'll be proud to care for him anytime."

John turned the horse toward the county courthouse, which was downtown facing the city square. The courthouse and city jail were in the same building. John was too late to be of any help. The sheriff and two deputies had been able to quell the riot and cool tempers enough to return the neighborhood to normal.

Two white men were in the jail, charged with disturbing the peace. There had been some shots fired on both sides and some injuries, but no deaths. Old Doc Mills patched up the gunshot wounds and put a cast on the arm of one of the prisoners who was hit in the upper arm. A court date was not set so there was no need for John to remain. He rode out to the ranch to spend some time with Max and visit old friends among the ranch hands.

After John left, Sally went to the liquor cabinet and opened a new bottle of Southern Comfort New Orleans whiskey. Before noon she had consumed more than half the bottle and had fallen asleep with the bottle in her lap, out until midafternoon. After three hours of sleep, she continued drinking until that bottle was empty.

She continued drinking with fitful naps for the next two days and nights. There were only trips to the washroom to relieve herself, then she returned to the bottle. During the wee hours of the third night, she shot herself in the right temple with the .32 Derringer she always kept near. John never learned of the death of his mother, having been told she had died when he was born and having no reason to think otherwise.

CHAPTER
XVIII

A few weeks following the shooting, Bonita realized she was pregnant. Devastated, she had no idea what to do. She knew it was possible but very dangerous to have the child removed from her body. There were old Mexican women she had heard of who could cause her to lose the child but she didn't know how to ask to find them. She prayed that the child would simply die and leave her body.

With no hope, she went to the mission and talked to Father Diego. In the confessional, she sobbed as she talked: "I am with child by the bandito," she cried. "Must I have this evil thing? What can I do? I am all alone. I cannot have a child. Please, Father, what can I do?"

"The sin is not yours, my child," he said. "You have done nothing wrong, but it would be wrong for you to destroy this life God has given to you. The father of your child was not killed. He lives now and stays here."

Bonita gasped. "He is here? He didn't die? I'll kill him. He is the devil and should go back to hell." She stood and started to leave the confessional.

"No, stay, child," the priest said. "Have faith and God will give you strength. God has given this man life, and we may not take it from him. There is a purpose. I will help as I can and will ask our friends to help you through this trial."

The priest went on for several minutes as Bonita sobbed uncontrollably in the confessional. His words were of little comfort and she interrupted him after a time. "Bless me, Father, and pray for me," she said. Still crying, she rushed from the chamber and returned home.

The priest had convinced the girl to have the child, and she continued to live in the small home her parents had built before their murders. Ham struggled to get back on his feet, but in the next three months, he was able to stand and soon was able to take a few steps.

The next six months were torture for Bonita, as her body swelled and her breasts became tender, as if stung by bees. An older Mexican woman with nine children came to be with her when the time came for her to give birth.

For a first child, the birth was surprisingly easy. After only three hours of labor, the top of the child's head appeared, then a few minutes of excruciating pain, and the child was born. A boy, well-formed and complete.

The older woman clipped the umbilical cord and tied the remaining cord as tightly as she could against the baby's skin. Bonita lay in exhaustion as the lady tended to the child. After he started breathing and let out a small cry, she held him by the ankles in one hand, head down, as she cleaned him.

She wrapped the baby in an old sheet and placed him beside Bonita. "Take it away," Bonita cried. "I don't want it. I don't want this devil child. Get rid of it. Do something with it." Tears poured from her eyes, and she could not stand to see the child as memories of the rape flared in her mind.

After a short time, with the old woman soothing the child, Bonita fell into a fitful sleep with crazy dreams of the child becoming a grotesque beast. For almost a year, she had suffered because of that monster. As dawn broke, she roused and got out of bed. The old woman was sleeping quietly beside the bed, sitting in an old rocking chair.

Bonita gathered the child, still wrapped in the old sheet, stole quietly from the room, and walked the short distance to the mission, the child in her arms. Quietly, she entered the mission and headed through the chapel into the sanctuary.

There, sleeping in the bed usually occupied by the priest, was the man who had used her so cruelly. "Here, gringo bastard," she screamed and almost threw the child atop the startled man. "This is your bastard child. Take him and both of you go to hell where you belong."

The baby was crying now, and Father Diego, having been sleeping nearby on a pallet on the floor, rose to see what was happening. It was clear what had transpired, and he wrapped his arms around the girl. "Please, my child. Calm yourself," he said.

She surrendered to the comfort of the priest's arms and stood limply as he held her. The child continued to cry, and Ham had nothing to say. Clumsily, he held the child above him as the baby continued a desperate, screeching cry.

"Please, child. Care for the baby," the priest said as he held Bonita against his chest. The cries of the baby melted her heart, and she could not stand it. Disentangling from the arms of the priest, she retrieved the child and tried to soothe him. The baby continued crying, and after a few moments, she exposed a breast and touched the baby's lips to her nipple. Through whatever instinct God had provided, the child realized the nipple was what he wanted and needed.

In only a few seconds, the cries stopped as he took the first meal of his life. "Oh, Jesus!! What am I to do?" Bonita cried. Tears flooded from her eyes as she watched the child nurse. Ham watched, dumbfounded.

Confused and not understanding what she wanted nor what she was to do, she left the sanctuary and returned home. Ham was ashamed the priest was aware of what sort of a man he had been, and tears came.

"I didn't mean to hurt the girl," he said. "It's just one of those things. Men do things like that. I didn't mean to hurt her. I never thought of hurting her. I sure didn't want to give her a child." He could not hold back the tears streaming down his cheeks. But his confession was cleansing to his soul.

—⁕—

Chapter
XIX

Ham recovered enough to start helping Father Diego with simple chores such as cleaning the rectory and chapel and working in the courtyard to clear around the tombstones.

The nights were cool, and he tried walking outside the compound. He was slow with the homemade crutch under his left arm. The right arm, still useless, lay in a sling across his abdomen. But he enjoyed the exercise and gained strength enough to be of use to the priest.

The pain in the left leg was constant, but in time Ham became accustomed to the pain and was able to ignore it. Working in the graveyard to remove the weeds, he learned to bend his good knee enough to kneel, place the crutch within reach, and accomplish most tasks with his left hand.

Born naturally right-handed, it was difficult to transition to his left hand, but he had no choice. He ventured outside the walls of the mission only at night and avoided people as best he could.

It was a long walk for him from the mission to the home of Bonita. He would stand for an hour or more at some distance from the house. After the girl inside blew out the light, he would creep closer and leave a gift for her, an orange or some bread from his meal at the mission. Usually it was food of some sort, but when there was no food to be had, he would bring a small bouquet of flowers or a trinket of some sort, like the small doll he had carved from mesquite wood. Once he found a dollar lying in the street and took it to her back door, hanging it from a string where she could not fail to see it in the morning on her way to the outhouse.

The months passed and Ham adjusted to the point he was able to work in the girl's small garden. On clear nights, by the light of any moon better than half, he pulled weeds, mounded the dirt around the vegetable plants, and brought manure from the neighbor's barnyard to nurture the plants. Bonita had one of the best gardens in San Benito, with vegetables growing all year in the fertile soil. She knew it was Ham doing all these things for her, but she never spoke to him. She still feared him and despised him for what he had done to her. The boy, who she had named Diabolito, was a handsome child and easy to care for, always happy and playful.

Ham was working in the garden one night after dark when two young Mexican boys came to the house. There was a loud commotion as the boys forced their way into the house. Their purpose was clear to Ham, and it quickly became clear that the girl could not control the boys.

"Don't fight, whore," one said in Spanish. "You made a baby with a gringo, and now we're going to give you a real baby with good Mexican blood." The smaller boy had a firm grip on Bonita's arms, and the older boy grasped the top of her dress, ripping it to her waist.

Ham burst through the door in a rage. Charging toward the trio, he was a wild man. With one long hop on the crutch, he reached the boy in front of Bonita and struck with all his might as the boy turned toward him. Blood spurted from the boy's flattened face as he fell.

The younger boy, in fear of this crazy person, released Bonita and prepared to defend himself.

Balancing on his right leg, Ham swung the crutch, striking the boy in the head. As the boy fell backward, Ham hopped forward on his good leg, raised the crutch, and jabbed the boy viciously several times in the crotch. The boy would not be interested in any form of sex for some months—if ever again.

Bonita ran from the room, and Ham stayed as the boys struggled to get up. In fear of losing their lives, they scrambled toward the door before the madman could do more harm.

As Ham left to return to the mission, Bonita spoke from the darkness: "Gracias, Piggy. Gracias."

"De nada," he replied.

Ham continued to work with Father Diego and stay at the rectory, sleeping now on a makeshift bed he had made himself from scraps of lumber. He fashioned it with sturdy legs of small logs cut from the mesquite trees outside of town.

There was much land being cleared and leveled to become productive farmland in the valley, leaving the gullies lined with trees, brush, and patches of cattails. There were still many cacti, and the sand burrs were troublesome. Horned toads scrabbled here and there in the loose soil in search of something to eat. Rattlesnakes were plentiful, and snakebites were frequent but rarely fatal.

Work on the system of canals was one of the few opportunities for men to find work outside of farm labor. Jobs became more available as the government got more and more involved. As water became more available, the citrus industry grew rapidly along with vegetable farming.

Bonita's child grew to look to Ham as a father figure and spent a lot of time with him. As the years passed, she, too, relied more and more on Piggy to care for the child.

Recovered to the most extent possible, Ham was able to do odd jobs in the neighborhood to earn a few pennies—seldom more than a dollar and normally no more than ten cents, occasionally a quarter. The pay was usually given out of pity more than for the task performed.

With the generosity of the priest, he survived, living at the mission. He contributed what he could in addition to the chores inside the compound. Mission San Benito was only the structure, and the property was surrounded by a wall built of stones with a rear gate large enough to allow the passage of a horse-drawn hearse, giving access to the burial grounds. One of Ham's duties was to help the priest make large bricks of mud and straw mixed with bricks of clay found on the banks of the nearby river. Also mixed with tough weeds for strength, they were excellent building blocks that lasted far better than bricks of clay alone.

From the time the boy was five or six years old, he spent most of his days with Ham, helping as he could to accomplish whatever tasks were set before them. When the boy was twelve, Ham saved enough to buy him a .22 single-shot rifle; he bought it for a dollar from a child in need of money.

With a box of .22 short shells, he took the boy outside the village for lessons in handling a weapon. After half a box of shells, Ham stopped the practice. Shells cost money and money was difficult to come by. A box of shells cost thirteen cents, but the shopkeeper sold them two boxes for a quarter.

When the boy was fifteen, Ham took the pistol and pistol belt from a Mexican bandito who had been shot by one of the landowners. It was a long-barrel .38 Colt revolver with a gold-plated trigger guard. The boy was delighted and wanted to go immediately to the gully where they had practiced with the .22.

The only ammunition available was the loaded gun plus the ten rounds in the gun belt. The boy was permitted to fire the six bullets in the weapon, but Ham said he should save the rest for later.

As the child grew up, he became known as Dio, and his given name was seldom used. Dio found work, and in addition to helping his mother, he earned enough doing odd jobs to buy an occasional box of cartridges for the pistol. With Ham as his mentor, he became proficient in the use of the gun.

At eighteen, he wore the gun belt anytime he left the house; this was not uncommon in the area during those turbulent years. Mexico was in turmoil and many Mexicans were coming north to escape the fighting. Dio was sympathetic and helped those he could to find shelter and food.

There were few jobs available in the area that paid enough to live on. Conditions were better farther north. Dio urged the ones he met to keep going, even though the next hundred miles or more would be very difficult.

Dio was eighteen when he heard that a Texas Ranger was in town, staying at old Mrs. Johnson's rooming house and asking about Ham. Knowing nothing of the gunfight in which his grandparents had died, he spoke to his mother.

"Men at Mrs. Johnson's are askin' about a man called 'Ham,'" he said. "I heard someone call Piggy 'Ham' once. I think it was Mr. Brown at the store."

CHAPTER
XX

Ranger John Welder was well known in South Texas, from Houston to Brownsville and as far west as Del Rio. Fort Worth had become a well-known and prosperous cattle town, and one of his chores was to visit the stockyards there to check for stolen cattle.

He became an expert in recognizing an altered brand. His judgment was seldom questioned, and the seller normally accepted the ranger's judgment and relinquished the animal to the original owner with no recrimination. John made mental notes, and on subsequent trips, he could recall that a seller had tried to sell altered brands in the past. Also, it was more suspect when a seller had more than two altered brands in his herd.

During the spring, John enjoyed some time off to visit old friends at the ranch and spend time with Max. He rarely saw his dad at the ranch, but saw him more often in Austin, where the elder Welder kept an office near the capitol. Texas Ranger headquarters was only a stone's throw away from there. Young John was well liked among his peers as well as with the senior commanders.

He was promoted to captain and was the youngest captain in the Rangers at the time he was given command of D Company. D Company encompassed all of South Texas, including almost all of the Rio Grande Valley. At lunch with a group of businessmen in Corpus Christi, he heard tell of a bandit in the valley who had been shot some years ago but had survived and was living now with a priest in an old mission.

Details were scarce, but the story interested John. *Could it be possible the man he had left to die had actually recovered and still lived?* After the lunch meeting and spending two additional days in Corpus, John rode south to San Benito.

Once more he stayed at the widow Johnson's rooming house. At breakfast, he broached the subject. "Heard stories ... Ham is still alive and living with the priest?" he asked.

Mrs. Johnson watched John's face for some time before responding. Was it just idle curiosity or was there some hidden purpose? "He's still livin', John." She paused. "And yes, he is staying at the mission. Took him a long time to recover, and he's still a broken-down cripple. Turned his life around after you shot him up. Good Christian man now and we're lucky to have him livin' here. Works hard. Can't do much, bein' all stove up, but he does the best he can. I use him myself when I need help around here. I'm gettin' too old to do some of the outside stuff, and he grows some good stuff over at Miss Credo's garden. I buy from him. Always picked fresh and nothing but the best."

It was obvious to John that she was defending the bandit and thought he was reformed. Without comment, he finished his breakfast, strapped on his gun belt and left the house. Walking to the store, he bought a box of shells for his pistol and another for the lever-action Winchester he carried on the saddle. As he paid for the shells, he spoke to the store owner.

"Heard the bandit called Ham wasn't killed in that shootin' a few years back. Is that true?" John asked.

The merchant, too, studied John's face. "You look familiar. I was here when that took place. You the man who shot him, ain't you?"

John turned and leaned back against the counter, elbows resting on the countertop. "Yes, that was me. I was on my own back then. Didn't get into the Rangers until later. I was just down here on business, hiring wetbacks for my dad's place."

The merchant came from behind the counter to talk to John. "I remember that gunfight like it was yesterday," he said. "They call him Piggy now or some just say Pig. You pushed his face into some pig shit and that girl shoved his face in it, too. She said something like 'Die, pig' or something like that. Maybe it was 'Go to hell, pig.' Anyhow, the name stuck."

The merchant was excited to meet the man who shot Ham, eager to relive the moment. "He's a changed man now. Been livin' with the priest in the old mission. Does stuff around town to make enough to pay for his keep. Takes care of that little girl he shamed. She's got a boy about grown. They call him Dio, but she named him Little Devil or something like that in meskin."

John was in no hurry to leave and stayed to visit with the merchant. "Been a Ranger now for quite a while and ain't never left a mess like this. Had no idea until just now that the bastard was still livin'. You can pass around that I'll be cleaning up my mess before I leave town. No need for him to leave town or hide. I'll find him."

The merchant, having accepted the crippled man as a part of the community, attempted to change the ranger's attitude. "Pig's not a bad sort. Just a crippled old man now. Does what he can to get by and don't bother nobody. Takes good care of that girl and just about raised the boy. Everybody knows it's his boy, and he's done right by the boy. Tried all he knows how to make it up to the girl. I think Bonita has got over what he did to her. Put it behind her, so to speak."

He went on, trying to convince John that it was not necessary to kill the man. "Scum like that got no place if people want to live in peace," John said. "He'll lie, cheat, or steal to get what he wants. Don't change what he is because he's pulled the wool over everybody's eyes. I'll give him till noon to face me and then I'll go lookin' for him."

With that John left the store, walking past the mission and on down to the boardinghouse.

Chapter
XXI

After entering through the back door of the rooming house, John took a seat at the kitchen table. "Mrs. Johnson, could I have another cup of that coffee, if you ain't thrown it out?"

"I keep coffee on all day, John. Some want coffee all times of the day. I'd rather see a man drinkin' coffee than hard liquor. Got some that put liquor in their coffee at breakfast." She poured coffee in a white mug for John and half a cup in a teacup for herself. "You're looking all worked up, John. What's troubling you?" she asked.

"Just somethin' I gotta do before I go back north. Left a mess down here several years ago. I'll be leaving town this afternoon, but I'll be here for dinner." At Mrs. Johnson's, she served "breakfast, dinner, and supper."

The merchant had wasted no time in letting the priest know that John was looking for Ham. Father Diego went to talk to Ham, who was cleaning the chapel. "There's a ranger in town," he said. "Says he's looking for you. You been in any kind of trouble you haven't told me about?"

Ham looked totally dejected. "I know what it is," he said. "He's come to kill me. He thought he killed me before. You saved my life but I'm sure he thought I was dead. Must have found out I was still alive. That's been a lot of years ago. You know I've lived a clean life ever since. I've tried all I know how to make up for my sins, and the only way for me to get past this is to face it. Been working with Dio, and I'm still good with a six-shooter, even with my left hand. If this is my time to meet my God, so be it. I'll finish up here and go look him up."

The priest stopped him. "No, my son. More killing is not the answer. God will protect you," he said. "I'll go talk to the ranger. I know he will listen to reason. You have changed your life and you need do no more to deserve redemption for your sins. God is your judge and this man has no right to condemn you. Do not leave the sanctuary of the mission. He will not enter here. This is sacred ground."

The priest left to find the ranger, and as he walked toward the rooming house, he saw Bonita, a package in her arms. He said to her, "My child. There is a ranger in town who has demanded to see Pig."

Bonita dropped the small package she had been carrying. "What does he want?" she asked. "Piggy has done no wrong."

He took her arms and looked into her eyes. "He plans to harm him. Perhaps even kill him. It is the same ranger who shot him many years ago."

"Oh, no!" she said. "He is not the same man. I have forgiven him for his sin against me. He is a good man now. The ranger has no right to harm him now. I'll go talk to him."

The priest released her. "No. I am going to see the ranger now. I'll talk to him. Go to your house and stay inside. Find Dio and tell him to stay inside. I'll do whatever is necessary to stop this evil."

Dio was at home when she arrived. He sat at the kitchen table working with his gun belt, rubbing neat's-foot oil into the leather. "Dio! Thank God you are here. You must stay inside because there is a ranger in town who plans to harm Piggy."

Dio stopped working with the leather belt. "What's a ranger got to do with Pig? Pig's not done anything wrong."

"He's the ranger who shot your papa years ago." It had never been a secret that Ham was Dio's father, but the two had never acknowledged a father-son relationship. They had always known each other as just Dio and Pig, yet even Dio had known from early childhood that Ham was his dad. Such a secret would have been impossible to keep because everyone in town knew of the time the Credos had been killed and that a baby had been born following the rape of the child Bonita.

Ignoring the priest's command, she left the house to look for the ranger. Dio quickly finished working on the belt, checked the gun to be sure it was loaded, and prepared to face the ranger himself rather than see his beloved Pig slaughtered. As he walked down the dusty path, he nervously practiced a fast draw several times.

Dio had known there could well come a time when he would face another man. In the culture of the times, it was better to die than to be known as a coward. Ham had taught the boy that fear was a good thing. Fear sharpened the senses and sped up the body.

"Fear is only bad when you let fear control you," Ham said.

As Bonita ran toward Mrs. Johnson's, she saw the priest entering the old mission. She burst into the rooming house where Mrs. Johnson was in the kitchen, preparing the vegetables she planned to serve at the noon meal. The ranger had just left.

Bonita turned and hurried to the mercantile store. The owner was behind the counter. "Please, I need a gun!" she cried. "There is a crazy man in town! He plans to kill Piggy! Help me!"

The merchant, well aware of what was happening, reached beneath the counter and brought out the twelve-gauge shotgun he kept there in case of trouble. He kept the gun loaded with #4 shot. Bonita took the gun and ran toward the mission.

There, ahead of her on the dusty road, was the ranger. To the right was her son, coming up the road from the river, gun in hand. Past the ranger, she could see Ham, walking toward the ranger with the crutch under his right arm, walking awkwardly to keep his left hand free to use his weapon.

John walked slowly now, some twenty paces separating him from Ham. He watched closely for any movement from Ham. To even touch his gun would be excuse enough for John to kill the man in self-defense. Ham made no move to draw his weapon; his left hand remained hanging loosely by his side.

In frustration and with only fifteen feet or less between the two men, John started to draw when a shot rang out. The shot came from the bell tower above the mission. The priest had shot the ranger, using the Sharps rifle Ham had left in the mission.

Bonita ran past the fallen ranger. Dropping the shotgun, she clutched Piggy in her arms and sobbed. "Piggy, Piggy, I was so afraid." As she held him, Dio arrived and joined in the hug. After a few moments, they turned to look at the ranger lying on his back, shot through the chest.

The priest came from the mission and ran toward the body on the ground. "My God!" he breathed. "What have I done? A mortal sin! I've killed. God forgive me!" He knelt beside the body and started to clean the ranger's face. "How can I be a man of God?"

Tears ran down his face. There was no sign of life in the body beside him. Ham, with Bonita on one side and Dio on the other, returned to the Credo house. The merchant returned to the store, cranked the telephone, and asked the operator to put him through to Ranger headquarters in Austin.

It took several minutes for the operator to make the connection. The ranger on duty took the message: "There has been a shooting and Ranger Welder has been killed." The ranger had difficulty understanding. "I'm having trouble hearing you," he said. "Who did the ranger kill?"

"No, no. The ranger is dead; the ranger is dead. Ranger Welder was killed." There was a long pause.

"Did you say Ranger Welder is dead? Ranger John Welder?"

"Yes. Yes. That's right. John Welder was shot about noon today. He is at the old mission in San Benito. The priest will bury him here."

The ranger on duty scrambled up. Holding the phone, he yelled at the secretary, "Get Major Jones!" Within minutes, the news had circulated throughout headquarters and the governor had been notified.

CHAPTER
XXII

As soon as he heard the message, Governor Davis called John Welder. "John, I've got some bad news," he said over the phone. "No easy way to say this, John. Your boy has been shot and killed. Some little town down in the valley."

John had feared for the boy's safety since he first joined the Rangers. Seemed like every day of a ranger's life was filled with danger. Texas was a lawless place during those years of staggering growth. The war in Mexico precipitated frequent incursions across the border by Mexicans desperate to avoid the conflict at home. With few opportunities for the young men flooding in, frequently, and in desperation, they turned to crime.

"Governor, could I use your rail car and a locomotive to get down there?" John asked. "I'd like to bring my boy home, back to Victoria, and have a proper burial."

The governor was quick to respond. "I'll tell them down at the station to get the car ready with a full coal car and an extra crew. They will have it ready by the time you get to the station. You can be in Brownsville before daybreak tomorrow."

John shuffled the papers on his desk. There was nothing urgent that required his immediate attention. "Miss Simpson!" he called to his secretary in the outer office. "I've got to be gone for a few days. I'll probably be gone all next week." He rushed back to the rooming house, gathered a few things in a bag and hurried to the train station.

It had been close to two hours since the governor had called and was late afternoon when he arrived at the station. The engineer greeted him, saying, "We're ready to go, Mr. Welder. The governor had them clear the track all the way to Brownsville. I'll run her as hard as I can. Sorry for your loss. You sit back and I'll have the steward bring you anything you'd like."

His mind in turmoil, John had difficulty concentrating. After a few minutes, with the train under way, John got up and paced up and down the governor's luxurious private car. Three men sat quietly in the front of the car; they were the extra crew that would relieve the crew on duty in four hours.

The crew knew the route well and pushed the engine well past the usual maximum speed. The trip from Austin to Brownsville on a normal run would require twelve to fifteen hours with the normal station stops. There would be no stops on this trip. After an hour, John was beside himself. "Can't you speed this thing up?" he yelled at the backup crew.

"The boys are pushing it pretty hard, Mr. Welder," one of the crew said. "I'll go talk to the engineer. I don't think he can run it much faster and be safe." He watched Welder, and it was clear the man was desperate to get to his son.

He went forward, crossed the coal car, and spoke to the engineer. "Mr. Welder wants you to push it up some, Steve. I know you been running pretty hard but maybe another five miles an hour would be OK." The engineer, already tense at the unusual speed at which he had been running, was concerned. "I've been pushing her harder than I should. I'd really be riskin' a derailment if any faster."

As they talked, the train approached the bridge over the Guadalupe River. A mile or so before the river crossing, there was a slight curve to align the tracks with the bridge. An older bridge across the river had been replaced with a new bridge some twenty yards up river. As the engine made the turn, the engine left the tracks and plunged to the riverbank below.

As the huge engine plunged off the tracks, the coal car, acting much like a whip, threw the passenger car completely over the engine and into the river below. All three men in the passenger car were killed as well as the engineer at the throttle.

The second engineer and the coal tender survived the accident but sustained severe injuries. Both died before daybreak. They had been pulled from the wreckage by local citizens.

CHAPTER
XVIII

The headline in the *Victoria Advocate* the next day covered the entire paper above the fold. In bold letters, the paper proclaimed, "EXTRA." Below that, in only slightly smaller letters: "TEXAS RANGER KILLED." Below the fold, it said, "LOCAL RANCHER DIES IN TRAIN WRECK."

The printer was not capable of printing enough newspapers to satisfy the demand. People gathered outside the newspaper office hoping to get a copy. The editor posted a notice on the front door: "ONLY ONE COPY PER CUSTOMER." Those lucky enough to buy a paper were quickly offered huge profits if they would sell their copy. Many were resold for a dollar each.

There was little in the paper not associated with the two tragedies. One full page recalled the amazing life of the elder John J. Welder, with many references to his exploits all the way back to his youth and studies at the Virginia Military Institute. He was lauded for his amazing vision as founder of the first frozen meat shipping business from the Texas coast. Stories of his venture into ranching and daring gambles as an investor in railroads were retold. It seemed everything he had touched turned to gold, much as King Midas in the legend from Greek mythology.

Bud Galloway called for a meeting of the board of the bank. Welder had been the senior member, president of the bank, and owner of a controlling interest. It was difficult to calm the six remaining members of the board. *Where do we go from here?* they all wondered.

Welder had had more than a million dollars in his personal account, with a checking account containing almost a quarter of a million dollars, certificates of deposits of another three million dollars, and more than twenty deeds of trust in his own name that the bank administered.

Galloway opened the meeting of the board with, "We've got a really bad dream here." The members burst into loud and excited conversations, all attempting to be heard. Galloway was unable to silence them for a minute or more. All the members had a financial interest in the bank, and for some the assets of the bank were their only net worth. Some owned rather expensive homes that were financed by mortgages through the bank. "Who are the heirs?" "Who do we have to work with?" "Is he married?" "Has he got any children?"

Bud calmed the members once more. "I'll tell you what I know, and some of it ain't good news," he started. "John was married. There were two children, John M. Welder and Patty Welder Welder. That is her legal name. John's wife was Charlene Beck Welder, and she died almost two years ago. John M. was shot the day before his dad died. J.J. came here after the war, and as far as I know, he had no other family here or up north." The board was deathly silent.

Most knew the story from village gossip: John had banished his wife, and some knew of her enterprise as a madam of a house of ill repute.

"That can't be right," Stewart Frels offered. "John sent her away and they weren't married any more. That girl ain't got no claim on the estate."

Everyone was silent, hoping that what Frels had said was true. But if it were true and there were no heirs, the bank would still have a hell of a problem sorting out all the legalities with the state of Texas. For sure the state and federal governments would have their hands out.

Galloway spoke again: "I'd talked to John about that more than once. I don't know why he never made it legal. I guess he thought it was enough that he had banished her, but there never was any divorce. He never asked her for one, and far as I know, he never spoke to that woman after she left the ranch."

Again, there was a loud discussion as each tried to express his opinion—all talking at once. "I ain't had time to make up my mind, and I move we hire some high-powered outside legal counsel to advise the board about all this," Galloway said. None on the board had a better idea, and after only a few minutes of back and forth between the members, all agreed to get someone who specialized in law specifically as it applied to banks and lending institutions. That option would cost some good money, but the members all agreed that it should be done. None were interested in becoming involved in any lengthy lawsuits.

Galloway called a friend in the Federal Judicial Center for information about the best legal minds in Texas regarding banking matters. "Best legal mind in Texas, far as I know, is retired now," the man said. "Judge on the Court of Appeals for fifteen years or more. I don't think you can find anyone better."

Galloway took down the name and where the judge could be found. He turned the information over to his secretary and asked that she locate the judge and get him on the phone. It took her almost an hour to locate the judge in Waco. Galloway took the phone and said, "Judge, this is Bud Galloway in Victoria. I've got a dilemma at the bank here, and I need some legal advice."

Judge Locke responded, "I'm retired now. Haven't been practicing law since I left the bench. What kinda problem you got?"

Bud spread his notes before him for reference. "I have lost a member of the board of directors, and he was a major member of the board. Board president in fact. He's been killed, and as far as we can find out, he ain't got any clear heir to his estate. Mr. Welder was married, and the only survivor in his family is a daughter, but the girl was not raised by Welder, and her claim could be disputed. It's complicated."

The judge interrupted. "Is that John Welder? Father of the ranger who was killed down at the Rio Grande by a Mexican priest?"

Bud was relieved. "Yes, that's the same man. We can't be sure the girl has a legal claim to his estate, and we can't find any other heirs."

There was a pause. "If I look into that, it could take a month or more. I'd need to go through some records at the courthouse in Victoria. I knew John from some cases that came before the court. As I recall, they were to do with railroads. Property rights and that sort of thing."

"That's OK, Judge. We just want some advice before we jump in and do something stupid."

"I'd take a look, but it will cost you. I'd want all my expenses paid, and I'll give you my advice in writing. It'll cost you five thousand dollars plus all my expenses. You won't have any guarantee that any court will agree with what I tell you. If you can agree to my terms, I'll get to work on it tomorrow."

Bud slumped in his chair with a sigh of relief. "Thanks, Judge. That's fair and we'd like you to start right away. We'll wait until you tell us the best course of action before we even talk to the girl."

The next two weeks, Judge Locke pored over birth records and marriage records and talked to all the people he could locate, both in town and at the Welder ranch. At last he talked to Patty. She told him about her life as far back as she could remember.

She had grown up in the house she lived in now, where she was working as a prostitute. She could not remember a time she had not lived there, nor a time her mother did not entertain men. She knew from childhood that her mother was a whore and that she had always had other ladies working. There had always been a maid, and the same Negro lady worked for her still.

She had known Max Stone, because he visited her mother frequently. He was always friendly, and she knew him as Uncle Max. She had no secrets and was open about her life and how she was raised. She had not had any close friends in school, and as she got older some of the kids teased her about her mom.

The judge could find nothing to indicate in any way that Charlene had not been married to John J. Welder, and there was nothing in any of the records that indicated that John or Charlene had ever talked of divorce, nor had there ever been any legal documents to show the marriage had been terminated. It was his judgment that Patty Welder

Welder was the daughter of John J. Welder and had been raised to believe her name was Patty Ride.

The judge could find no indication in any of the records or in conversations with those who had known John Welder for years that any other relatives existed. He submitted his report before a meeting of the board of directors.

After the presentation by the judge, Galloway spoke to the group: "I don't think we have any choice. We best break the news to Miss Welder now. She may well be the richest woman in Texas, and she owns a controlling interest in this very bank. Let's take a break. An hour from now, I'll listen to anyone who doesn't agree."

The board members left the room and Bud stayed with the judge. "I'll take care of your bill now, Your Honor. We appreciate your time and effort. I think we did the right thing by getting an opinion before doing something inappropriate." With that, Bud wrote out a check for the services plus personal expenses not previously paid.

"I can cash that check if you'd rather have cash, Your Honor," Bud offered.

"No, I'd rather not carry that amount while traveling. I'll just deposit the check back in Waco."

The two shook hands and Bud had his secretary gather any documents having any references to the John J. Welder account, anything at all that contained a reference to Welder. The package filled a briefcase-size folder. When the board reconvened, there was little discussion regarding the course of action.

Chapter
XXIV

Bud picked up the phone and asked the operator to please get Miss Patty Ride on the phone. "Hello," she said when she answered.

"Miss Ride, this is Bud Galloway at the bank. There seems to be some problems with your account here at the bank. Could you please come in and discuss the matter with me?"

She hesitated. "I hope I've not made a mistake. I hope I'm not overdrawn?"

"No, no. Not at all, Miss Ride. I'd rather not discuss it over the phone, but it is important that I talk to you personally."

"Has this got something to do with that man asking all the questions? Some sort of a judge? He sure asked a lot of questions."

"Yes, I don't know if he told you, but he was working for me. It is nothing you've done wrong, but I do need to talk to you, face to face."

"I'm not busy. Should I come up now? It's about a fifteen-minute walk. I'll bring my checkbook."

Bud asked the other board members to wait for her arrival. He felt all should be in on this discussion. When Patty arrived, Bud was in the lobby to welcome her. "Please come with me," he said, as he guided her to the interior of the bank.

His private office was at the entrance to the conference room, and he steered her to a chair in his office. "I have some shocking news for you, Miss Ride. I don't know what your mother told you about your family before she died. Do you know what your mother's maiden name was or who your father was?"

"No," she replied. "Mom never talked about any family. Only family I know of is my Uncle Max. He lives on a ranch out east of here. I think the Welder spread. He would probably know more than me. He visited my mom a lot. Not a customer, just a friend." She made no attempt to conceal her occupation nor that of her mother. "I never talked to Uncle Max about family."

Bud watched her closely as she talked. "This is really difficult, Patty. Did you know that your real name is not Ride? Your real name is Welder. You were delivered by old Doc Mills. Your mom left your dad before you were born. It's all in the public records at the courthouse."

Patty sat wide-eyed as Bud talked. "Good Lord! You tellin' me that I was, am, John Welder's daughter? Is Max his brother? Max is still alive. I've seen him. I don't know Mr. Welder. Don't think I ever saw him. Why are you tellin' me all this?"

Bud was hesitant. "I've got to tell you this. Your dad is dead and your brother, John Max Welder, is dead. Your brother is, was, a Texas Ranger and got killed in a gunfight. Your dad was on the way to care for his body when there was a train wreck west of Goliad and he was killed."

Patty was confused. She hung her head in thought for close to a minute before looking up. "So, I need to take care of the funeral and all that? Is that why you wanted to talk to me?"

"No, there's more than that. I think your Uncle Max has taken care of that. Your dad and brother were buried two weeks ago at the Welder ranch. You are the only heir to the Welder estate. Both your dad and your brother had extensive holdings."

Patty sat in silence, unable to absorb all Bud was saying. "I'm sorry, I just don't understand.

What do you want from me? What has all this got to do with me and my banking here?"

"What this means is that you own all that your dad and your brother owned. In all, it is quite a fortune. I'll make room for you here in the bank and help you through all this if you like."

Still confused, she asked, "Room in the bank? Why would I need room in the bank?"

"Miss Welder, you own this bank. You have some partners in the bank, stockholders, but you have the controlling interest. By rights, you are chairman of the board of directors. You also own all the holdings in land, stocks, bonds, cash, and everything else your dad and brother had."

Patty was in shock. "I feel sick, Mr. Galloway. Could I lie down? I think I'm going to be sick."

Bud guided her to the couch against the wall of his office, and she stretched out. He brought a wastebasket and placed it on the floor beside her head. "That's just in case, Patty. I'll give you some time, and when you feel better, we'll talk some more. It's going to take a long time to get through all you need to do. Just rest for a bit and we'll talk some more."

With that, Bud left the office and went to talk to the board members, still waiting in the boardroom.

"Y'all go get some dinner, and we'll meet back here this afternoon about two. The girl is feeling poorly and needs some time. All this comes as a complete surprise to her."

Patty had no experience in business beyond running the house of ill repute. Her home was paid for, the girls worked for half their earnings, and the maid, Minny Bell, worked for two dollars a week plus room and board. She had accumulated a substantial amount in her checking account, but this was a total change in her life.

She accepted the offer of an office in the bank. Bud had the handyman equip the office with as good or better furniture and decor as his own office. The education started immediately, with the head teller responsible for guiding her and answering any questions she might have.

She asked the priest at the mission on the south end of Main Street to conduct a memorial Mass for her dad and brother. She wanted all the patrons of the bank to be invited to attend the services. Bud made it clear to all associated with the bank that the invitation should not be ignored. It would be an opportunity for the most influential citizens in the area to meet Miss Welder. Some, mostly the ladies, were inclined to skip the services and avoid expressing condolences to Patty. Her previous activities were well-known, and most were reluctant to welcome her in the new role of "wealthy widow."

Later Patty made arrangements to purchase the Wheeler mansion on North Main Street, an imposing Italian-style, southern European villa. There was a high stone wall with stucco veneer surrounding the mansion and grounds. The entrance off Main Street sported ornate cast-iron gates made of spikes, with some five inches between spikes. The gates remained closed at all times and required a footman to open them from inside the walls.

In spite of her new surroundings and obvious wealth, Patty was not accepted into the largely closed society of wealthy families in the area. Settled into the mansion, she gave title to the house on Commercial Street to the lady who had been so loyal and had cared for her all her life, Minny Bell.

The house operated as before under new management. The most noticeable change was there were now two light-skinned Negro girls working. The local gentlemen called the girls "mulattos" or "high yellers," and they were very popular with the clientele.

Patty tried as best she could to win favor with the local citizens. She continued to entertain the young men of the best families in an effort to gain entrée to their friends and families. The young men, as well as two or three married gentlemen, enjoyed her company. Businessmen warmed to the attractive lady and were not reluctant to do business with her. In her new position as president and chairman of the bank, she attended the town meetings and those of the Victoria County Merchants Association.

During one meeting of the town council, the subject of inadequate school facilities came up. Patty asked to be permitted to address the school board at their next meeting. She was introduced at the meeting by the president, and after a brief opening, in which she declared her support for better education of "our children," she made a dramatic offer.

"As chairman of the board at the bank and in the name of the bank," she stated, "we will donate the eighty acres on East Street as a location for a new school. The land is now property of the bank, having completed foreclosure. The land will be free and clear. In addition to the donation of the land, I will personally pay for the construction of a new school building. Whatever design and at whatever cost the Victoria School Board decides."

The room burst into thunderous applause with yells of "Bravo! Bravo!" *Finally*, she thought, *this should give me some standing in the community.*

CHAPTER
XXV

Unfortunately, the good ladies of the community were not persuaded and continued to shun Patty. As could be expected, she became more and more frustrated. *What would it take to force them to accept me and forget my past?*

She had settled into her new lifestyle but had no real duties at the bank. Perhaps some time away? she thought. She checked with a travel service and decided on an extended vacation to get out of sight for a few seasons. The Grand Tour of Europe seemed like a good plan.

She made arrangements with an architectural firm from San Antonio to design and construct a mansion on her property that would be the envy of all of Texas. The firm would be in control of the entire enterprise, both of removing the existing Wheeler mansion and constructing a completely new home on the property, one that would be highly visible on Main Street where the north-south highway crossed. The highway was the main artery between Houston and the Rio Grande Valley and was heavily traveled.

Having made all the necessary arrangements, both with the architect and with the bank, she prepared to travel. The land holdings were in good hands, with Uncle Max in full control. She authorized Bud to make all the payments to expedite the work on her new home in her absence.

The tour was more exciting than expected, and she enjoyed Paris so much that she rented a small apartment near the River Seine and learned enough French to communicate awkwardly in that tongue.

Through the concierge, she arranged a three-week cruise on the Seine. *This will show those stuck-up whores*, she thought. *I've done things they have only dreamed of.*

After arranging for the shipment home of all her European purchases, she traveled overnight by train to Athens. While in Athens, she got word by wire that the work was nearing completion on her new home, and the contractor needed more instructions to complete the work. Personal preferences in colors, choices of fabrics, and landscape and gardening ideas would be difficult for her to choose from a distance.

Patty arranged for the shipping of the things she had bought in Athens and booked passage on the ocean liner, *Confederate Queen*, docking in Savannah, Georgia. From Savannah, she booked a luxury private car to take her to Victoria. From the ship, she sent a long telegram to Bud Galloway asking that he arrange a reception at the train station for her arrival.

The crowd at the station to greet her was much larger than expected. All the people in the area had been watching the progress as the Welder mansion was under construction. Covering most of four normal-size city blocks, the mansion was truly impressive. Constructed primarily of brownstone, it had fences made of the same stone enclosing the entire estate. A four-story structure with cupolas, it had a tower above the third floor that was accessible by a spiral staircase.

From that viewpoint, Patty was able to see all of the city of Victoria. The finish work and furnishing the mansion took another two months following her arrival. Nearing the Christmas holidays, she planned a Christmas celebration at the mansion.

All the elite in Victoria County were invited, with some invitations to important people from San Antonio and Houston.

Both architects were invited with their families to be introduced at the party. It was not only a party to celebrate the birth of Christ, but it also was a showcase for the interior of the palatial estate, which had drawn visitors from miles around to view the amazing mansion.

The party was well attended since many of the invited had obligations to the bank and could not ignore the invitation. The grand ballroom was packed. Waiters dressed in specially made Christmas costumes moved through the crowd, replenishing glasses and offering delicacies on silver trays. The gentlemen in the crowd made their way to shake hands with Patty and wish her a merry Christmas.

As one of the young men was making small talk, his date rudely said, "Let's get out of here. This place looks like a high-class whorehouse." She made no attempt to prevent Patty from hearing her words.

Mr. Taglabue, a friend (and satisfied former client) of Patty's, was standing nearby and spoke loudly enough for the departing couple to hear clearly. "Who'd ever have thought that young lady had ever been in a high-class whorehouse?"

Patty, not expecting the remark, burst into uncontrollable laughter. The gathering became very quiet as the partygoers attempted to learn what the commotion was about. In all, the party was a success and Patty was satisfied she had finally broken through with the majority of the citizens in the community. With some unimportant exceptions, they seemed to have accepted her and only rarely displayed their previous disdain and even contempt for her.

She only went to her office in the bank occasionally. When she left the mansion, it was almost always in the chauffeur-driven carriage, a 1900 Horch touring car, a handcrafted, one-of-a-kind automobile shipped to her from Germany. She sat regally in the center of the rear seat, elevated slightly for a better view.

One beautiful spring day, returning to the mansion after time at the bank, she had the driver stop so she could speak to a young man she recognized. Willie Jenkins, son of the local meat packer, had moved to Victoria to manage a subsidiary company for his dad. Patty invited him to ride with her and, if he cared to, have dinner with her at the mansion. He was delighted to do so and eagerly accepted.

Well aware of Patty's history and reputation, he accompanied her to the mansion—having never had the opportunity to check whether she actually did the things gossiped about her. They made small talk and she offered a glass of tea while waiting for her cook to prepare the dinner. He sat on a couch and she sat beside him as they talked.

Once, as she was making a point, she placed a hand on his leg for emphasis. At the touch, he involuntarily jumped but then settled back, her hand still in place on his leg. Aroused now, it was difficult for the young man to complete the meal. Mrs. Atwell, the cook, brought goblets of brandy following dessert of glazed peach slices. As Patty sipped the brandy, she suggested they take a tour of the house so she could show off her collection of *objets d'art* and other features of the mansion.

She took his hand as she led him through the mansion, making small talk and telling of her travels. As she talked, she related interesting sights and people she had seen during her tour of Europe.

"The European people are far more advanced than Americans," she said. "They are more liberal in their views, and it's not unusual for a married man in Europe to also have a mistress."

As she spoke, they entered her bedroom, which featured a custom-made bed covered with fine linen. Willie was beside himself. By now it was obvious that it would not be a seduction on his part; she was clearly ready to take him on the oversize bed. She sat on the side of the bed and touched the bed beside her, inviting him to join her.

She turned toward him as he sat and offered her lips. They embraced and she started to unbutton his shirt. The young man was frantic now, overcome by the passion that had been building for almost two hours since she first offered the ride in the automobile. The first joining was overly eager on Willie's part, and he completed far too soon for her satisfaction.

They lay back, Patty cuddling in his arms as they rested. "That was great," she lied. "I've been dreaming of making love to you since we first met." She lied again.

"I've always wanted you, too," he said. "I didn't think you even noticed me." They rested awhile before becoming intimate again. The second time, Patty was both impressed and satisfied with the performance of the young man.

It was nearing sundown by the time Willie moved to get dressed. "Willie, you are doing very well, and I could help you with your business. It could be of great benefit to you and your company to have the capital you need to expand. You could be the largest meat-packing company in Texas."

Willie was confused. "Why would you be interested in something like that?" he asked. "You've got all the land you can handle and more money than you can ever spend."

She lay back, still totally nude. "I was thinking it was time I became an honest woman. I'd make you a good wife, and I'd make you richer than you ever dreamed of being."

Willie stared at the woman, not believing what she was offering. "I could never marry you, Patty. My family would go totally berserk if I ever even thought of marrying you."

It was a stab to her heart. "So, I'm just fine for a roll in the hay but not good enough to be a wife?" She got out of the bed in a rage, threw a lamp from the stand beside the bed, and cursed,

"GET OUT, YOU BLOWED-UP SON OF A BITCH!! Get out of my house!"

Willie, still fumbling with his belt buckle, ran from the room and down the stairs. As he burst out the front door of the mansion, the chauffeur rushed to open the gate for the young man. "Have a good evening, sir," the chauffeur said as Willie departed. He could not suppress a grin as he watched the man walking swiftly toward town. *That'll teach him to rile Miss Welder*, he thought. *Must have been a disappointment to her in bed.*

Patty pulled on a gown and climbed the stairs to her "alone place" in the tower. She carried the bottle of champagne from the canister, placed there by the maid; it was cooled but unopened. She sat, looking out at the town, and popped the cork from the bottle, sipping the bubbles from the bottle as they spilled over in a sparkling cascade.

She sat for an hour drinking the champagne and watching the sun set over the town to the west. In time the bottle of champagne emptied, and she dropped the bottle to the floor. Making her way in the dark down the spiral staircase to her bedroom, she walked to the veranda, which faced east. She pulled a chair to the balcony rail, stepped up onto the chair, then on top of the balcony rail. Her last step was into the air over the flagstone patio three floors below.

The End

—⁓⁓—

Acknowledgments

Special thanks to the libraries of South Texas for their open-arm welcome, and for allowing me to research past events in history.

ABOUT THE AUTHOR

Roy Calvin Moore was born in San Benito, Texas, in March of 1932. The seventh of ten children the family struggled to survive The Great Depression. Growing up, he spent hours listening to the "Old-Timers" tell of the hard times in Texas following the Civil War. There were also stories of huge fortunes made by land purchases when land was selling for as little as two cents per acre. Characters of all walks of life would scramble to this area for a piece of the American dream. This is the history that inspired him to write.

Roy entered the United States Air Force in the Fall of 1949 at the age of seventeen. When the Korean War began, the Air Force was desperate for pilots and he rose to the challenge. He entered pilot training as an aviation cadet and was commissioned as a second lieutenant in the fall of 1954. During that training, he met and married Joan Hatton.

His years of service allowed him to see the world living in such places as Okinawa, Philippines, France, Spain, Turkey, Libya, and England. He was awarded the Top Gun trophy in 1968 while flying in Spain. With this achievement, he was assigned as Instructor Pilot to the top-ranking officers in the Sixth Air Force and the 401st Tactical Fighter Wing.

Never having lost interest in the history of Texas, he spent hours in the public libraries as well as the newspaper archives in South Texas. This book is the product of twenty years of work in hopes of capturing the ambiance of that era and the history of South Texas to the readers.

Made in the USA
Columbia, SC
05 April 2020

90847792R00119